TROUBLE
at
TIMPETILL

TROUBLE at TIMPETILL

Henry Winterfeld

Illustrated by William M. Hutchinson
Translated by Kyrill Schabert

AN ODYSSEY/HARCOURT YOUNG CLASSIC
HARCOURT, INC.
San Diego   New York   London

www.HarcourtBooks.com

First Harcourt Young Classics edition 2002
First Odyssey Classics edition 1990
First published in the United States in 1965

Library of Congress Cataloging-in-Publication Data
Winterfeld, Henry.
Trouble at Timpetill/Henry Winterfeld; illustrated by William M. Hutchinson;
translated from the German by Kyrill Schabert.
p.   cm.
Originally published: San Diego: Harcourt Brace Jovanovich, 1965.
"An Odyssey/Harcourt Young Classic."
Summary: When the Pirates, a gang of young boys in the small town of Timpetill,
become too rowdy, the adults decide to discipline them by
leaving the town in the middle of the night.
[1. Behavior—Fiction.   2. Self-reliance—Fiction.]
I. Hutchinson, William M., ill.   II. Schabert, Kyrill.   III. Title.
PZ7.W766Tr   2002
[Fic]—dc21   2002024380
ISBN 0-15-216306-9   ISBN 0-15-216274-7 (pb)

Printed in the United States of America

A C E G H F D B
A C E G H F D B (pb)

Contents

TROUBLE
at
TIMPETILL

1

Never Tie Things to a Cat's Tail

Willy Stolz never should have tied the alarm clock to the tail of Peter the cat. The consequences were fatal.

Of course, Willy belonged to the Pirates. What a crazy gang! Surprisingly, quite a few girls belonged to it, too. Scarcely a day passed without the Pirates being up to some crazy business in our little town called Timpetill.

One night they smashed all the streetlights on Main Street, and everybody had to find the way home in the dark. Another time they turned on the fire hydrants on the very day the farmers had come to town to sell their produce. It caused a deluge like the Flood. Baskets filled with vegetables floated away, three chickens and two rabbits were drowned in their cages, and one man's candy canes all dissolved. The grownups were furious. But you can never catch these Pirates. Willy Stolz is the worst; otherwise, he would have left Peter alone. One should never tie things to a cat's tail. That's a mean trick.

Not even Willy, however, could have foreseen the consequences of this deed. I happened to be standing at the window of my room looking down on Old Square. I saw Willy stealing up to Peter. The cat, curled up, was drowsing peacefully in the warm midday sun on a bench in front of the butcher's store, probably dreaming of all the beautiful, fat sausages that were hanging in the window. Willy tied the alarm clock to Peter's tail with such skill that the cat never woke up. This was quite a remarkable accomplishment; not even an Indian could have improved on it.

Needless to say, Willy had not forgotten to wind up the alarm. I was curious to see what was going to happen. Suddenly, the alarm went off right next to Peter's ear, and he leaped high into the air, turned a few somersaults, and then, like greased lightning, bolted across the square. The alarm clock, firmly tied to his tail, bounced behind him, still ringing shrilly. At this moment, Mr. Kroeger, the postman, was turning the corner into the square on his bicycle. In his panic, Peter jumped on Mr. Kroeger's head, and the clock hit the postman on the back. Mr. Kroeger bumped into a lamppost, he fell off his bicycle, and all the letters flew into the gutter. Peter

raced on toward the pharmacy, where Hans, the apprentice, was standing on a ladder in front of the shop, washing the window. Peter shot up the ladder and, in a frenzy, dug his claws firmly into Hans's back. Frightened out of his wits, Hans lost his balance, the ladder started to teeter—and Hans and Peter with ladder and bucket hit the pavement. As bad luck would have it, Miss Line, the old spinster, was standing in front of the pharmacy. She got thoroughly soaked, shrieked, and passed out in a dead faint. That was all Peter needed. He darted into the pharmacy. A terrifying crash came from inside. It sounded as though the entire furnishings had been smashed to smithereens. Mr. Tropp, the pharmacist, dashed out, his white jacket flopping. He wrung his hands and cried, "This mad animal is ruining me! Ruining me!"

I watched Mr. Tropp run to the fire alarm box and smash its glass pane. Then I dashed down the stairs, three steps at a time, shot through the front door, and ran across Old Square to the pharmacist's to catch Peter before he managed to wreck all of Timpetill. Peter, however, had already emerged from the pharmacy. He darted between my legs and rocketed straight across the square, the clock still dangling from his tail. Then he leaped through a window of the Town Hall to land smack in the middle of Mayor Lomser's office.

Meanwhile, people came running from all directions and gathered around Mr. Tropp.

"What happened? What's going on?" they asked excitedly.

"That crazy animal is my ruin!" cried Mr. Tropp.

"What animal?" asked the people anxiously. They

probably were thinking of bears or boars, which were rumored to roam in the nearby forest.

"It was a big black tomcat," complained the postman, pointing accusingly to his damaged bicycle and the soiled letters.

Suddenly someone shouted, "Fire!"

Thick smoke clouds belched from the pharmacy. Peter must have knocked down some chemicals, which had exploded.

From a distance one could hear the siren of the volunteer fire brigade. It was none too soon; flames were bursting from the window.

The grownups were petrified. The children were happy. At least something really exciting was happening! Willy Stolz was nowhere to be seen; prudently, he had vanished.

Mayor Lomser appeared on the steps of the Town Hall. In his right arm he held Peter, and in his left fist he clutched the alarm clock. Peter looked a bit ruffled, but otherwise happy. He was rid of the instrument of torture that had been tied to his tail, and to him that was all that mattered.

"Whose cat is this?" shouted the mayor across the square.

"Mine, Mr. Mayor," cried the butcher, Mr. Stettner.

"Did *you* tie the alarm clock to his tail?"

"For heaven's sake, no," protested Mr. Stettner.

"It must have been those naughty children again," squeaked the old spinster. She was still sitting on the sidewalk, surrounded by concerned neighbors.

Mayor Lomser set Peter free and angrily sent the alarm clock bouncing down the steps.

"The cat jumped through the window onto my desk and knocked over my inkwell. A lot of documents are ruined. I've had enough of these outrageous pranks. We must teach our children a lesson they will never forget," barked the mayor.

"Yes, we must," echoed the other grownups, and turned around to glower at us. We children thought it best to disappear as fast as possible.

2

Enter Thomas

I ran to find my best friend, Thomas Wank, who lives on Hill Street. He is the son of our cobbler and often helps his father repair shoes. Thomas was sitting on a stool near the open shop door, pounding wooden pegs into a boot. Mr. and Mrs. Wank were not at home. Apparently, they had joined the infuriated parents in Old Square. The Wanks had only recently moved to Timpetill. Before, they had lived in Kollersburg, where Thomas had been a Boy Scout leader. Now he was in the same class with me, and we had become friends.

"Thomas," I cried, "our parents want to get rid of us!"

Thomas dropped his hammer. "Professor, have you gone nuts?" he said.

My friends call me "professor" because I wear glasses and like to read. My name is Michael Freeman. I am thirteen years old and live on Old Square, where my father owns a stationery store. I want to become an inventor, and that is why I love to read books about science, especially physics. I am quite good in math.

"No, Thomas," I stammered. "Honestly, they have sworn to get even with us. This time they mean it." I told him what had happened.

"Ha, ha!" Thomas laughed. "Don't get excited. We didn't do anything. It's always the Pirates."

Thomas and I didn't want to have anything to do with the Pirates. Not that we are such angels, but we considered them and their so-called heroic deeds silly. That's why they can't stand us.

"But our parents don't know about the Pirates," I said crossly. "We're all the same to them. They think all the kids in Timpetill have gone stark-raving mad."

"Hm," muttered Thomas. He got up from his stool. "Come along," he said with determination, and ran out into the street.

I followed him, puzzled. "Where are you going?"

"To the Pirates," he said.

That puzzled me even more. "Why to the Pirates?"

"I want to tell them that all Oscar wants is to make more trouble. It's time someone put an end to this whole Pirate business—it's silly."

Oscar was the leader of the Pirates. He is the son of the butcher, Mr. Stettner, and we call him Bloody Oscar. His overalls are always bloodstained because he has to help his father carry the meat into the store.

"Aren't you afraid?" I asked.

Thomas stopped. "If you want to back out, I'll go there by myself. Why don't you creep into a mousehole, meanwhile?"

"Oh, I'll come along," I replied.

It was getting dark, and we quickened our steps. As we reached Linden Street, we ran into Mark Himmel.

"Have you heard?" he called excitedly. "Our parents are having a big meeting. They're planning something awful."

Mark is thirteen. He is slight and not very strong for his age. His face is covered with freckles, and some of the children tease him because of them. Thomas and I are his protectors, and anyone who wants to make fun of him has to put up with us.

"Do you have any details, Mark?" Thomas questioned him.

"No, unfortunately. When our parents looked at us so threateningly, I climbed the chestnut tree next to the Town Hall and hid. All the parents went into the Town Hall with the mayor. They sounded as though they had something terrible in mind. All of a sudden they began to whisper like conspirators, and I couldn't hear anything any more. I jumped down from the tree and ran to warn you. Where are you going now?"

"We're going to the Pirates," I said casually.

Mark's eyes popped. "Great Scott! How come?"

"Thomas wants to tell Oscar off."

"Let me come, too," Mark pleaded.

"Nothing doing," said Thomas. "It might be dangerous, and then you'd only be in our way."

I'm no coward, but I'll admit that just hearing Thomas's words made me feel a bit weak in the stomach.

We crossed a mowed field and climbed up the hill to Mill Street. Across the street was the meeting place of the Pirates, a vacant riding academy called the Arena. A rich man who loved horses had built it many years ago. But no citizen of Timpetill has ever owned a saddle horse, so the Arena now is always deserted and in poor condition. The children are the only ones who are really happy about it. It has a regular ring, surrounded by benches, and a wooden barrier just like a circus. Here the children play as jousting knights or bullfighters, and sometimes even as circus performers. The building stands in a garden overgrown with weeds. Actually, the children are forbidden to enter it, but they pay no attention to this rule. When the Pirates were organized and grew stronger, Oscar brazenly took possession of the Arena, and from then on only Pirates were allowed to enter it. Whenever they felt threatened, they withdrew to this hiding place.

We climbed the lattice fence and crept through the high weeds toward the Arena. The walls are red brick, and the narrow windows are covered with ivy. Many of the windowpanes are broken, and those that are not are so dirty that you cannot see through them. Part of the roof has collapsed.

The building loomed eerily in the dusk. It stands beneath towering spruce trees. The ghostly light of candles flickered through the windows. As we came closer, we could hear the muffled murmur of voices. The Pirates had a full turnout.

Fighting his way through brambles, Thomas reached the back door. He opened it as quietly as possible, and we entered. We stood pressed against the wall, not daring to move. My heart was pounding, and I would have loved to turn back, but rather than admit this to Thomas, I would have bitten off my tongue. The benches were crowded with boys and girls ranging from ten to fourteen years old. Their eyes were fixed on the ring. In the center of the ring, among the weeds that sprouted here and there, stood a crate. On top of the crate, stuck into some empty bottles, were three burning candles. Behind the candles, perched on a bench, sat the leader of the Pirates, Oscar, flanked by his lieutenants, Willy Stolz and Hans Lomser, the mayor's son. All three wore masks cut out of heavy wrapping paper, but I recognized Willy at once by his red hair. In front of Oscar lay a hatchet, which was probably now missing in his father's butcher shop.

Thomas grabbed my arm and whispered to me to keep still. He could have saved himself the trouble. I had no desire to make my presence known. "Stay where you are, Professor," he muttered, "no matter what happens. You've got to cover our retreat."

As yet the Pirates had not discovered us. The light of the candles did not reach as far as our hiding place. Oscar banged the crate three times with the hatchet, so that the bottles holding the candles bounced. Silence reigned.

"Pirate boys and girls," he barked, "our parents are foolish. They are sitting in the Town Hall wondering how to punish us. But they can't scare us."

"Right," Willy said, interrupting him. "How can we help it if a stupid cat suddenly goes raving mad?"

"What a nerve!" I said to myself, outraged. "It's because of him that we're all in trouble!"

Again Oscar banged the crate with his hatchet. "We'll show our parents where to get off. We won't go home tonight. We'll stay here all night. By tomorrow they'll be glad to see us back again."

"But we have to go to bed," said a boy who sat on the barrier. His name was Fritz Bollner, the baker's son.

"Mama's boy," sneered Oscar.

A few boys and girls giggled, but they sounded ill at ease. Lotte Dronte, one of the younger girls, raised her hand as if she were in school and said shyly, "My mother will be worried!"

"Let her worry," said Oscar, "but if you don't want to stay, go on home. We know how to deal with traitors."

"Traitors are our deadly enemies," said Hans Lomser ominously.

Lotte Dronte sank back in her seat and began to cry.

All of a sudden Thomas shouted, "We've had enough of this!" He hurtled over the barrier and stormed into the center of the ring. Raising his arms over his head like a boxer who has just climbed into the ring, he yelled, "Don't let him fool you, you blockheads! Oscar will get every one of you into trouble."

The children jumped up in fright. Oscar,

speechless with surprise, sat as if nailed to his bench. Thomas had appeared like a ghost from the grave.

"Go home, all of you!" Thomas called to the children. "Don't listen to Oscar. He is an idiot. Quit playing this silly game of Pirates. If you don't, you'll really be in hot water."

The children did not move. They were confused and embarrassed. Thomas's words were having their effect. But now Oscar emerged from behind his crate.

"I've been meaning to have a showdown with you for a long time, you conceited sissy," he snarled. He was about to hurl himself against Thomas, but Thomas jumped forward and hit him on the nose.

"Ouch," cried Oscar, and drew back. The mask had been pushed over his face, so that he couldn't see a thing. "Hans, Willy! Grab him!" he ordered, pulling at his mask. With marked reluctance, the two Pirates advanced from behind the crate. They knew that Thomas was stronger than they were.

In a moment, Oscar had pulled off his mask. Wild with rage, he lowered his head like a bull and charged at Thomas, intending to knock him over. Thomas stepped skillfully aside, and Oscar spilled, face down, in the sand. But he got back on his feet immediately and pummeled Thomas with both fists. Thomas hit back, and the fight became wilder and wilder. They began to wrestle, and Oscar tried to get Thomas in a stranglehold, but Thomas was too quick for him. By this time, all the boys were standing on the benches and yelling, "Let him have it, Oscar! Don't let him lick you. Trip him up!"

For the moment all fear of their parents had vanished.

The girls were terrified. "How disgusting," they cried. "Stop it, stop it!"

I was trembling for Thomas, but remembering my orders, I did not move from the back door.

Both opponents were now wrestling in the sand. First Oscar was on top, then Thomas. Soon they were on their feet again, their arms locked. Their shadows, flickering on the bare walls, looked like two giants engaged in a deadly struggle. All at once, Thomas got Bloody Oscar in a stranglehold. The Pirate chief was helpless. He tried vainly to kick Thomas. At that point, Hans and Willy started to sneak up from behind. "Look out, Thomas!" I shrieked.

Thomas whirled around and kicked over the crate. The candles fell into the sand, and suddenly it was pitch dark.

"Ouch, my stomach," I could hear Willy cry. Perhaps somebody had stepped on him. It served him right. But I could also hear a lot of boys jumping into the ring, probably to help Oscar. It was high time to pull Thomas out of the fray. What could I do? Desperately, I pounded the door with both fists and yelled as loudly as I could, "Our parents are coming, our parents are coming! Let's get out of here."

First, there was total silence, then screams and an outbreak of panic. The thunder of feet sounded like a stampeding herd of buffalo.

I could feel Thomas by my side. "Let's beat it," he panted, and pulled me along. We ran outside, jumped over the fence, and dashed across the field

like frightened rabbits. Not until we reached Thomas's house did we catch our breaths.

Thomas slumped down on a stool. "Ugh!" He groaned, rubbing a big bump on his forehead.

I took off my glasses and cleaned them. "Boy," I gasped, "you sure let them have it."

"I got my share," growled Thomas, examining his bruises.

"Never mind," I said, trying to cheer him up. "You finished Oscar off for good."

"You're wrong, Professor. He won't give in so easily. But I have to hand it to you. If you hadn't yelled, 'Our parents are coming,' you would have had to carry me home."

We laughed but stopped abruptly. Mr. and Mrs. Wank had appeared at the door of the room and were looking at us reproachfully.

"Good evening," I stammered.

Mr. and Mrs. Wank did not reply. This was not a good sign. Ordinarily, they were friendly and good-humored. Now they looked through us as if we were thin air and disappeared without a word into the adjoining room.

"What does that mean, Thomas?" I asked.

"Something's up," he muttered, and scratched his head.

"I thought your father would give you a licking when you got home."

"I bet you were looking forward to that," said Thomas. "I guess they must have cooked up something. Whatever it is, Professor, I smell trouble."

He was right.

My parents behaved exactly the same way. And later we learned that the parents of the other children had acted just as strangely that night. After fleeing the Arena in panic, the Pirates had scattered, and groups of them wandered through the streets. Bloody Oscar and his lieutenants had disappeared. Apparently, the chief of the Pirates was bathing his swollen nose in the cool waters of Timpe Creek.

At last, the other children went home. They were tired and hungry, and they feared the worst. But miracle of miracles, nothing happened to them. There were no scoldings, and there were no spankings. They sighed with relief and quickly got into bed.

But the next morning, a painful surprise awaited us all.

3

No Breakfast for "Fatso" Paul

I woke up with a start. The church clock was striking eight, and usually I am called at seven.

I jumped out of bed and with my left foot stepped on the tracks of my electric train. On Sunday I had put together a new section, using my bed as a tunnel. My toe hurt, and I hopped on one leg to the window to look at the church clock. As usual, I had forgotten to put on my glasses, and I couldn't see a thing. I hopped across the room and knocked over the station house. I was furious. A fine way to start the day! After much groping, I finally found my glasses on the floor behind the night table. Lucky that they were still in one piece, I thought, or I wouldn't be able to see the writing on the blackboard at school. That sends Mr. Manz, our teacher, into a fury. I felt more nervous by the minute. I was bound to be at least half an hour late for school, and Mr. Manz couldn't stand that either. I yanked the door open and called downstairs, "Mother, Mother, why didn't you wake me? Please hurry with my breakfast." I ran back to the bathroom and put my head under the faucet.

But there was no water. That was the last straw! Could the pipes freeze in the middle of a heat wave, I wondered.

It was only at this point that I realized my mother was nowhere to be seen. Nor did I hear a sound. Probably Father was already downstairs in the store. I knocked on their bedroom door. Perhaps my mother had overslept, though I had never known it to happen before—she was always the first one up. Nobody answered. I stuck my head in at the door, but no one was there. I ran through the apartment and downstairs into the shop. My parents had gone out. A fine mess, I thought. Where might they have gone so early in the morning?

I went back to my room and dressed. I took time out to put the station house back in place again, threw my school books into my bag, and dashed down the steps.

I was still more puzzled when I reached Old Square. What had happened? All the shops were closed and the square was abandoned. A few children were headed toward Church Street, where the school is.

I caught up with fat Paul Brandt, who was putting on his jacket as he ran. His hair was tousled and he looked upset.

"What's the matter?" I asked him.

"My parents have disappeared," he panted.

I stopped, dumfounded, and grabbed him by the shoulders. "Yours, too?"

"I have no idea where they are," he said sullenly, "and I didn't get any breakfast this morning."

We continued on our way. A lot of children were standing aimlessly in front of the school. The door was locked. They surrounded me excitedly. "Michael," they exclaimed, "our parents have disappeared, and the school door isn't open."

"That's funny," I said. "Our parents couldn't have suddenly vanished from the earth. They must be somewhere."

More and more children came up. "We have no idea where they are," cried Karl Benz.

"I didn't meet a single grownup on my way here," Fritz Helm told us. He lived quite far away.

Mimi Menken started to blubber. "They— they—probably just took off."

"Rubbish, Mimi," I said. "Don't bawl. Our parents didn't take off. That kind of thing only happens in storybooks."

But I was wrong. It had happened.

"Nobody woke me up this morning," reported Hank Wittner, the son of the postmaster. "Our house is empty, my parents are gone, the maid is gone, and they even took our poodle."

"Maybe they're hiding in the cellar," said Klaus Anker.

"I didn't dare look," admitted Hank.

"Don't talk such nonsense," I snapped. "Postmasters don't hide in cellars."

Everybody had a similar story. Nobody had been awakened or given breakfast, and all the parents had vanished. They had vanished with uncles and aunts, babies and toddlers, as well as grandparents.

Then I had a terrible thought. I remembered that no water had come out of the faucets. I jumped on the low stone wall of the schoolyard and shouted, "Kids, listen to me. Who washed this morning?"

There was an embarrassed silence.

"Let's have it," I said. "I've got to know. It's important."

"I got up too late," said Kurt Fels.

"I just forgot," admitted Pussy Beck.

"There was nobody there to remind us," whined Fritz Bollner.

I jumped down from the wall and made a beeline for the nearest house across the road. The house door was open, and I ran through several rooms into the kitchen. Karl Benz and Fatso Paul Brandt followed me; the others stayed behind. They didn't have the nerve to crash into a house without permission. I went to the sink and turned on the faucets. Not a drop of water came out.

"That's that," I said. "They've turned off the waterworks."

"Now we've had it," said Karl Benz.

"We'll die of thirst," grumbled Fatso Paul.

"We'd better keep this a secret," I warned them both. "Otherwise, there will be a panic."

"We won't say a thing," they assured me.

Outside, the others were waiting anxiously.

"Why did you run into the house?" several wanted to know.

"We wanted to see whether perhaps there were some grownups inside."

"Is anybody there?"

"Nobody," I said.

"What am I going to do if our parents don't return?" complained Rita Strauss. She had two younger sisters at home for whom she felt responsible.

The other children, too, were worried. They hung their heads and would have burst into tears, except they were too ashamed. Some had dropped their schoolbooks and were sitting on them. Mournfully, they gazed straight ahead. The houses on Church Street were like tombs. Today, not even the closed school door was a cause for joy. We could hear a cock crowing as though he were mocking us. I felt helpless. Somewhere our parents must have found a secret hideaway—but where, and why?

Just then, as good luck would have it, Thomas and Mark Himmel appeared at the end of the street.

"Hey, Thomas," I called, relieved. "Come quick. A terrible, terrible thing has happened."

"I know all about it," replied Thomas as he approached. "Mark and I have been walking around for two hours. We've looked in every nook and cranny."

"Well, and—" I asked anxiously.

"Kids," Thomas said solemnly, "the town is dead. There isn't a single grownup left."

The little square in front of the school grew as silent as the inside of a church.

I took my glasses off and put them back on again. "Have you been to the Town Hall?"

"The Town Hall?" Thomas asked, perplexed. "Why?"

"Maybe they're all there again," I said.

My words had an electrifying effect. "Hurrah, hurrah, they're in the Town Hall," the children yelled, and they ran to Old Square.

Thomas, Mark, and I chased after them. We finally overtook them. It must have been a strange sight to see all of us swarming across Old Square toward the Town Hall.

Thomas was the first to reach the stone steps, and he bounded up them. When he reached the front door, he stopped dead. A printed poster was stuck onto it. He tore it off and waved it high in the air.

All the others stopped in their tracks. First, there was wild confusion, but at last there was silence.

Mark and I stood next to Thomas at the top of the steps. I could look across Old Square. Below us, the children stood shoulder to shoulder, gazing up. But there was something else I noticed—something that worried me a bit. Oscar, Willy, and Hank were coming down Main Street. They strode across the square to the statue and sat down on its edge with an air of defiance. On his back Oscar was carrying a huge sack, filled to bursting. I couldn't make out what it was, but I suspected he was up to no good.

Thomas had not yet noticed the Pirates. Squinting his eyes, he was studying the poster. Our parents must have had it printed during the night.

"Boys and girls," he announced, "our parents have left a message for us."

"Read it, read it," everyone shouted.

Thomas cleared his throat and then began:

"To our delinquent children. Our patience has been exhausted. Lately, you have carried things too far. We have given up any hope of making you come to your senses. That's why we are leaving town for good. From now on, it is up to you to get along without us. Perhaps someday you will realize that parents exist for something besides being annoyed by their children.

The Parents of Timpetill."

Thomas fell silent and dropped the poster. Not a sound could be heard in the square.

4

The Rumble Begins

Thomas handed me the poster and pointed to the lower corner. There, scrawled in red paint, it said, "Good riddance. Oscar."

I tore the poster into bits and threw the pieces to the wind. They whirled above the children's heads, high in the air, and then came down like snowflakes.

The children remained in a state of shock. They stared up at us as though the message from our parents had been a bad joke.

"I don't believe a word of it," said Robert Pell, the skinny son of the town judge. "Tomorrow my father is supposed to be in session."

"And it's washday for my mother," cried Lily Brown.

"The day after tomorrow we are expecting the painters," said Hank.

"Surely our parents will come home by tonight," said Pussy Beck, but she sounded uncertain.

"Kids," said Thomas, "our parents have really gone. We must decide what to do."

"We'll play cops and robbers," called Karl Benz.

"Don't be stupid," Thomas snapped.

"Stupid, yourself," retorted Karl, offended.

Meanwhile, I had noticed something I did not like at all. Bloody Oscar was standing on the pedestal of the statue glaring at us menacingly. I pulled Thomas's sleeve and whispered, "Something is going on back there."

"Oscar! I bet you that means trouble," he muttered.

Suddenly, Willy Stolz blew a toy trumpet, and Hans Lomser shot off a cap pistol. The children looked around, bewildered.

"Boy Pirates and girl Pirates," Oscar shouted, "come over here."

"Hurrah, Oscar!" and almost half the children ran to him.

"Pirates," barked Oscar, "our parents have run out on us for good—and, as far as I'm concerned, that suits us just fine."

His face broke into a broad grin. The children laughed and clapped their hands.

I had to hand it to Oscar. He really knew how to make the kids listen. While he was speaking, the rest of the children went over to him, and suddenly

Thomas, Mark, and I found ourselves alone at the top of the Town Hall steps.

"Our parents will never return," Oscar was saying. "Great! Now the whole town is ours. Now nobody can tell us what to do—and we'll do exactly as we please."

"Shut your big mouth," Thomas yelled angrily. "Kids, come back here."

"Don't listen to that double-crosser and his friend, the teacher's pet." Oscar sneered. "They just want you to be good so that they can have everything for themselves."

"I'll get him for calling us double-crossers and teacher's pets," I muttered, grinding my teeth.

Now the Pirate chief called, "Oscar wants you to be happy. Oscar is Santa Claus! Let me have the sack, Willy."

Willy held the bulging sack up to him. Oscar dug into it with both hands and then flung candy canes, cookies, and marshmallows into the crowd, which produced a shout of delight. The children fought for the goodies like hungry wolves.

"Thief!" Thomas was outraged, but no one paid attention.

Oscar made the most of his advantage. "This was only a starter, kids! Now we're off to get more.

Dolls, tin soldiers, balls, and popguns—anything your hearts desire."

"Hurrah!" the children shouted.

Oscar jumped down from the pedestal of the statue. "Let's go. Follow me," he commanded.

"Stop," Thomas shouted. "You can't plunder the town!"

He wanted to run across to Oscar, but Mark and I grabbed him and held him back.

"Leave him alone, Thomas," I urged.

"There's nothing we can do!" Mark pleaded with him.

Oscar had stopped. "Beat up those weaklings, somebody," he ordered contemptuously.

"Beat them up! Beat them!" shouted the Pirates, surging toward us. Stones began to fly past our heads.

"We'd better get out of here," I exclaimed hoarsely.

But it was too late. The first wave of attackers was already coming up the steps.

Thomas shoved off the leader, then quickly whirled around and tried the latch of the Town Hall door. It turned—we squeezed through the door, slammed it shut behind us, and leaned against it. Fortunately, the key was in the lock, and Thomas turned it. Outside, the children banged on the door

with their fists and feet, but before long they grew tired and went away. We stood in the dark hall, not daring to move. I looked out through a colored glass window. Through the old-fashioned leaded panes, Old Square looked small and strangely distorted.

The children were running behind Oscar, who was waving the empty sack like a flag above his head. He turned into Main Street, where most of the shops are. The children quickly disappeared, and soon all we could hear was their shouting.

"Crazy cow," Mark Himmel said. "That was a close one!" He was as white as a sheet, and there were beads of perspiration on his forehead.

"I was afraid they would bust my glasses." I coughed. I didn't want to admit that my heart had been in my mouth when the children came rushing at us.

Even Thomas looked rattled.

"If the door had been locked, we would have had a rough time." His laugh sounded a bit hollow as he ran his fingers through his hair.

We sat down on a marble bench to recover from our fright. Besides, we didn't dare emerge from our refuge so soon.

Still dazed, we stared at the stone floor. Suddenly, we could hear howls and screams of triumph coming from the direction of Main Street.

"They've broken into the stores," I said.

"I wonder how they got in?" said Thomas. "All the shops are locked."

"You're right. How did they?" I said, puzzled. "Wait a minute, I've got it—Mr. Grump, the night watchman!"

Thomas and Mark looked baffled.

"The night watchman? What has he got to do with it?" asked Thomas.

"Mr. Grump has duplicate keys for all the stores," I said.

"Well, so what?" Thomas had still not caught on.

"Boy, are you dense! Peter Grump is his son and one of the Pirates. He must have taken the keys, and that's how they've gotten into the stores."

"Our parents will hit the ceiling when they find out tonight," said Thomas grimly.

"Do you really think that our parents will come back tonight?" Mark asked.

"Why, of course," replied Thomas. "They just wanted to scare us. Maybe they took the train to Kollersburg and will take the evening train back. Or maybe they went deep into Recken Forest, where we can't find them."

Our little town lies tucked between rolling, thickly wooded hills, far from any main highway.

"But what if they don't come back?" I interjected.

"Now you're the one who's dense. Stop and think. They left all their belongings behind."

"Hm." I growled stubbornly. "But maybe they won't come back until tomorrow night."

"Then we'll just have to wait," said Thomas.

"Fine," I said, "but what would you say if I reported to you most respectfully that all the water has been turned off?"

Thomas jumped up. "No water?"

"Not a drop, old man," I said, grinning. Evidently Thomas had not washed this morning either.

"Hold everything," Thomas said excitedly. He crossed the stone floor to the light switch and flicked it. Nothing happened.

"Now we've had it! There isn't any electricity either." Thomas looked scared.

"Maybe it's the fuses here in the Town Hall," I said.

"You'd better check that, Professor," said Thomas. "After all, you're the technical whiz."

We went into the basement to look for the main switch. The cellar was cold and dark. Fortunately, I always carry a flashlight with me. I directed the beam of light along the dank, bare stone walls. At last we discovered the box that contained the main switch and fuses. A label above each fuse indicated the room it served. First, I tested the basement fuse and then all the others. Each fuse has a piece of wire behind a small mica window. When the wire has melted, the fuse has blown. But they were all intact.

"The powerhouse isn't operating," I reported.

We returned to the lobby and sat down on the bench.

In the distance we could still hear the children yelling.

"Will we have to wait here all day?" Mark asked timidly.

"Could be," said Thomas. "We can't go home. If we cross Old Square, the gang will pounce on us again."

"There's a back door on Church Street," said Mark. "If the street is empty, we can run over to the watchtower and climb it to the top."

"What for?" Thomas and I asked.

Mark hesitated, as if he were a bit embarrassed. "It's lunchtime now. If our parents have gone into the forest, they're bound to be cooking something. Then we'd see a column of smoke, which would tell us where they are."

He fell into an awkward silence. Obviously, he was homesick for his parents. I knew how he felt. It's funny how little attention we pay to parents when they're around. But when they're gone for any length of time, we don't like it one little bit.

"No good," growled Thomas. "If our parents are in hiding, they won't be so stupid as to make a fire."

"But on the other hand, they didn't think of the duplicate keys," I protested.

"That's right," Thomas admitted. "Well, I suppose we could try the tower. There's no point in sitting around here, and, anyway, it's no fun."

We ran through a number of corridors and at last found the back door that Mark had mentioned. Thomas opened it a crack and cautiously peeked out to see if there were any children around.

"O.K.," he whispered.

We stepped out into the street. The light was blinding, and we had to squint. Church Street seemed peaceful. The wind whispered softly through the leaves of the linden trees. A few sparrows were happily twittering, and from the garden across the street came the contented bleating of Mrs. Twilling's goat.

But the peace and quiet were merely an illusion. In the distance we could hear the other kids carrying on as if they had completely lost their senses. We crept toward the tower in the shadow of the garden wall. On our way, we ran into Marianne.

5

Worse Than a Pack of Thieves

Marianne was just coming out of her house.

"Hi, boys!" She greeted us cheerfully.

Marianne is my cousin. She is twelve years old and wants to be a schoolteacher. That's why she works hard at school, and most of the time her marks are good. Her father, Kurt Jansen, is our dentist in Timpetill.

"Who's this?" she asked, looking at Thomas with interest.

Hastily I introduced them. "Marianne, this is my friend, Thomas Wank."

"Oh, really. So this is your hero you've told me so much about."

Thomas blushed.

"He looks quite normal." She laughed. Thomas laughed, too, and the ice was broken. I was glad she liked Thomas. I would have been mad if she hadn't.

"Do you want to come to the bakery with me?" she asked. "Imagine, I just got out of bed. Nobody woke me up. I want to get some blueberry muffins."

"Where have you been all this time? Don't you know what's happened?" I asked.

Marianne looked puzzled. "What do you mean?"

We laughed.

"Why do you laugh?"

"There are no muffins today," Mark said.

"Oh, well, then I'll get some rolls. I like them, too, and they always have rolls."

"There are no rolls, either," I said.

"Why not?"

"Because there is no longer a baker."

"Oh, dear. Bollner doesn't exist anymore? That would be awful!"

"Nobody exists anymore," I said, and told her what had happened.

Marianne was beside herself. "Good heavens! Can you imagine? Well, my parents will get an earful when they come home. Now I understand why Mummy told me last night that there wouldn't be any school today. I can't believe that they won't be back. Father has visiting hours tomorrow." She looked at us anxiously, her eyes wide.

"They're sure to come back," said Thomas.

"Do you really think so?" Marianne smiled at him gratefully. "Where do you suppose they are?"

"We were about to climb the tower to see whether they're hiding in the forest," said Mark.

"But you wouldn't be able to see them in the forest from up there."

"It's noontime," I reminded her, "and they will want to eat. Maybe they'll make a fire, and we'll see the smoke rising."

"Good! I'll come, too," Marianne exclaimed.

"Do you want to join us?" asked Thomas, smiling.

"Of course. Did you think I'd rather go and steal chocolates?"

We reached the tower and hurriedly climbed the steep spiral stairs to the lookout platform on top. It affords a view in all directions, but Mark had to stand on his toes in order to look over the high railing. We went to the north side of the rampart. From here we could look far out into the country. Directly below us clustered the roofs and gables of our little town. Over to the left, we could see the station and the station plaza. Farther out, where the houses were sparser, Timpe Creek wound its way through hills and meadows.

Behind the meadows, the forest begins, extending to the mountains on the horizon. The mountains lie beyond our frontier and belong to our neighbor country. The frontier runs right through the middle of the forest, along a small stream that usually dries up in summer. Border guards patrol the frontier, but it is not too difficult to sneak across.

There was no sign of smoke. Only an eagle or a buzzard kited lazily above the treetops.

"They aren't in the forest," Marianne declared, her voice betraying her disappointment.

"You can't be sure," I said.

"If they are," observed Thomas, "they're smarter than we thought. They were careful not to light a fire."

"How about going into the forest to look for them?" suggested Marianne.

"Not me," Mark protested. "It's too easy to get lost in the Recken Forest."

We heard a loud bang from the center of the town and ran to the other side of the rampart to look down on Old Square. What a sight we saw! The children were running around in wild confusion, like a throng of dwarfs gone mad. Laden with toys, new groups kept pouring into the square. Their trumpets, drums, and whistles produced a deafening cacophony. Some were blowing up balloons, and a shout of triumph arose each time one exploded. Red, green, and blue balloons were sailing past us across the town. Mr. Meyer's toy shop must have been completely cleaned out. A number of boys wore football helmets, and others had put on Indian headgear. Arrows whirred through the air, tomahawks were brandished, and near the statue stood a tepee. A wild horde in war paint was dancing around Robert Pell, who was lashed to a lamppost. A group of children was playing soccer behind the statue; others were playing badminton, and in front of the Town Hall someone had put up a ping-pong table. In the midst of this heaving mass, children were crisscrossing on brand-new bicycles, roller skates, and scooters. Some girls were pushing doll carriages, and others were playing ball, while smaller girls sat on house stoops, changing dolls' clothes. Old Square had never seen such goings on, not even at carnival time.

"This beats everything," I said.

"Their behavior is an outrage," Marianne said in disgust. "They deserve to have all their teeth pulled."

Thomas just scowled. Mark said nothing.

From our vantage point, we could see the goings on on Main Street, too. From Nisser's Motorbike

Shop emerged a motor scooter pushed by Oscar, Willy, and Hank. Once in the street, they tried to start it, but happily they did not succeed. Probably the gas tank was empty.

Inside another store window, we could see Pussy Beck and some other girls sitting behind sewing machines. It was a good thing that there was no electricity, or they might have gotten hurt. Next door was Kern's candy store. There the children pressed against the counter, four rows deep. Chocolate bars and boxes of candy, already torn open, were being handed down the line, and I saw Fatso Paul Brandt stuffing his pockets. On the opposite side of the street, where the optician Potz had his store, half a dozen boys were dragging a telescope in the direction of Old Square.

"They are worse than a pack of thieves," I said in disgust, turning my back to the spectacle.

Marianne was so infuriated that she yelled down from the tower. "Stop it, you thieves! Aren't you ashamed?"

Thomas pulled her back from the railing. "For Pete's sake, don't do that. Be quiet!"

Marianne looked bewildered. "Why?"

"They hate us because we won't join them," Mark explained.

"That's why we can't go home," I said. "We'd

have to cross Old Square, and then they would attack us again."

"Why don't you come to my house?" asked Marianne. "There's no one on Church Street."

"Not a bad idea," Thomas replied.

"I think it's a great idea," I said. "Maybe you even have something for us to eat. We're starved."

"There's bread, peanut butter, milk, and apples," said Marianne.

"Swell," Mark exclaimed with joy. He liked going to Marianne's. Her house was light and cheerful, and there was always something to eat.

Before we climbed down from the tower, Thomas made sure that nobody was around. We ran down Church Street like frightened rabbits. We had to be sure that the Pirates did not find out where we were hiding. Otherwise, they might ambush us.

Marianne ran ahead, her hair flying. Perhaps she wanted to show us that she could keep up with us. She was first to reach the house. "Oh, what a dope I am," she groaned, clapping her hand over her mouth in distress.

"What's the matter?" I asked anxiously.

"I slammed the door behind me when I left. It has a snap lock, and the key is in the house. Now we can't get in."

"Good night!" exclaimed Thomas in disgust.

"Don't give up so fast," I said. "Let me take a look at it."

I pulled a piece of wire out of my pocket. I always carry a piece of wire on me. You can never tell when it might come in handy. I bent the wire at one end and made a sort of pick lock. I stuck it into the keyhole, gave it a few turns, and suddenly the door opened.

"Well done, Professor," said Thomas. "You are herewith appointed king of the burglars!"

We stepped into the house. Marianne banged the door behind her, and Thomas put on the safety chain. "Let's not take any chances," he said.

We were standing in the lobby, which also serves as the waiting room for Marianne's father's patients. Marianne led us into the sitting room, where Thomas looked around with admiration.

"Pretty neat," he said.

Marianne had already vanished into the kitchen. She was rattling dishes and humming a tune. A few minutes later she appeared, carrying a tray with four glasses of milk, peanut butter sandwiches, and apples.

"Help yourselves," she said, nodding at us encouragingly.

We needed no urging and pitched right in. Since

our parents had left, we had not had a morsel of food.

I was just chewing on my first bite when the front doorbell started to ring frantically. Terrified, I choked—with a crust of bread stuck in my throat. Marianne, Thomas, and Mark also froze in alarm.

6

A Cavity in the Molar

The bell rang again.

"Who could that be?" I whispered, gasping for breath. I didn't dare cough.

"Perhaps it's the mailman," Marianne whispered.

Thomas shook his head. "Mr. Kroeger has flown the coop, too."

He got up, put his finger to his lips, and tiptoed toward the door. He looked through the peephole and returned quickly.

"Karl Benz is outside," he said softly. "He looks as though he's been crying."

"Shall I talk to him?" asked Marianne.

"Yes—but leave the safety chain on."

Marianne opened the door just far enough to stick her nose out. "What do you want?" she asked.

"Oh, oh, my tooth! I've got such a toothache," we could hear Karl Benz cry.

Marianne returned. "He says he's got a tooth-ache. Shall I let him in?"

"Wait," said Thomas. "It might be a trap." He opened a window a crack, stuck his head out, and looked around.

"Nobody's outside. We'll hide in the next room and then you can let him in."

Marianne ran back to the door, took off the safety chain, and let Karl in. She did not forget to close the door behind him immediately and to put the chain back on.

"Oh, oh, my tooth!" whimpered Karl.

"What's the matter with your tooth?" asked Marianne, and wrinkled her nose scornfully.

"It hurts," squealed Karl Benz. "Ouch, ouch!"

"Why does it hurt?"

"Because! Is your father home?"

"My father took off with the rest of them," said Marianne.

Karl collapsed in an armchair. "But it hurts so!" he cried.

"He's not faking," Thomas said to us as we watched from the next room. Karl Benz buried his head in both hands and continued to wail.

"Stop your crying," said Marianne a bit more kindly. "Don't act like a baby. Come with me. Maybe

I can help you." She led him to her father's office. Thomas, Mark, and I followed them.

"Sit down." Marianne pointed to the dentist's chair.

"Why?" Karl Benz was alarmed. He looked around for a route of escape. Then he saw us and paled. "It's you!"

"I guess you don't like that," said Thomas.

"Just sit down on that nice chair, there," I said.

"It—it doesn't hurt anymore," he stammered.

"Coward!" Thomas gave Karl a shove, and he slumped into the dentist's chair. "Only this morning you were the big hero."

"Honestly, it doesn't hurt anymore," he repeated.

"They always say that," Marianne said with a superior air. She had put on her father's white coat. It was too big for her, but she rolled up the sleeves. She was holding a silver instrument with a small, round metal mirror at one end.

"Open!" she ordered him.

Taken by surprise, he opened his mouth.

"Which tooth hurts?" she asked.

Karl Benz pointed to one of his molars. Marianne shoved the instrument into his mouth, while we watched with great interest. She nodded, satisfied. "You have a cavity in that molar," she said.

"Does it have to be pulled?" Thomas asked casually.

Karl Benz wanted to jump up, but we had an iron grip on him. He squirmed frantically and croaked something. Marianne kept pressing the instrument against his tongue.

"It would be best to pull it," said Marianne, "but I haven't got the strength to do it."

"Oh, then let me do it," Thomas said eagerly. "I'm used to pulling out nails from shoes." He gave us a devilish wink.

"Help!" gargled Karl. "Please don't pull it! Let me go."

"Quiet!" snapped Thomas. "The doctor is in charge here."

"I think I can help him without pulling it." Marianne had the air of a famous professor. She poked around in her father's instrument cabinet and finally chose a thin silver rod with a small sharp hook. Skillfully, she poked it into the hole in the molar. Karl jumped as if struck by lightning, but we kept our grip on him. Marianne withdrew the instrument and pointed to a tiny dark brown lump at its end.

"Chocolate," she said scornfully.

We roared with laughter.

"It serves you right!" Mark shrieked gleefully.

Marianne filled a syringe with some liquid and

washed out the cavity. Karl groaned. Then Marianne pulled out some absorbent cotton with a pair of tweezers and stuffed it into the hole. She tapped Karl lightly on his cheek and said, "Finished."

We released our hold on him. He sat up and wiped the sweat from his face. Suddenly he made a face and grinned sheepishly. "What do you know? The pain is gone."

"There—you see," Marianne said proudly.

"Now beat it!" Thomas commanded icily.

We paid no more attention to Karl. Marianne took off the white coat, and we returned to the sitting room and our peanut butter sandwiches.

Karl Benz followed us. "Won't you let me stay here?" he asked timidly.

"What do you want?" I said.

"I'm through with the Pirates, Michael. Honestly. They've gone too far."

"So you're feeling guilty now?" said Thomas.

Karl nodded.

"Did you throw stones at us, too?" Mark wanted to know.

"I swear I didn't," Karl stammered. He looked scared.

"Why don't you just go home?" Thomas asked.

"But nobody's there. My parents are gone. I don't want to be all alone in the house."

Marianne intervened. "Let him stay, Thomas."

"OK, you may stay, Karl," said Thomas.

Karl leaped with joy. "Thank you, Thomas."

"Wait a minute," Thomas said. "First, you have to prove that you are on the level."

"What do you want me to do?" Karl asked eagerly.

"What became of the keys the Pirates used to open the shop doors?"

"They just left them in the locks."

"That's what I call a break," Thomas said cheerfully. "Go back to Old Square and get all the keys. But watch out that nobody sees you doing it. Then come right back."

"It's as good as done," Karl said, and started to leave.

"Hold it," I said. "How are you going to carry all those keys?"

"I don't know."

"I'll give him a bag," said Marianne. She handed Karl her mother's shopping bag. "Don't lose it," she warned him, "or I'll get an awful scolding."

"I won't," he said, and disappeared like lightning.

"I hope he'll make it," said Thomas. "If we get the keys, we can lock the stores early tomorrow morning when everybody else is sleeping. Then the Pirates won't be able to go on with their plundering."

"Marvelous," cried Marianne.

"Your plan is excellent, Thomas," I said, "but what if Karl double-crosses us?"

"He won't," said Thomas. But he looked worried.

Milk Is Delicious

Karl returned as he had promised. It had taken him a full two hours. He had all the keys with him, and he emptied the shopping bag before us on the carpet.

"What kept you so long?" Thomas asked, irritated. We had been on pins and needles all the time.

"It was tough to collect all the keys," said Karl. "I had to make sure that nobody was watching me."

"Thank you, Karl," said Thomas. "You did a great job."

Karl beamed.

Marianne gathered up the keys and threw them back into the bag. "I'll hide them in our house where nobody can find them," she said.

"Why?" I asked.

"You can never tell," she murmured, and glanced at Karl. I think she still didn't trust him completely.

"Thomas," said Karl, "Paul Brandt, Bob Pell, and Rita Strauss are waiting outside. They say they are fed up with the Pirates, too."

Thomas was elated. "Let them come in," he said.

Fatso Paul and Bob Pell looked a bit embarrassed. Rita was red-eyed from crying.

"What's the matter, Rita?" asked Marianne, alarmed.

"Lotti and Lisa are hungry." She sobbed. Lotti and Lisa are her little sisters.

"Isn't there any food in your house?"

"No. My mother was going to do the shopping today, but now she's gone all of a sudden," Rita said. "And my father, too," she added wretchedly.

"Why didn't you just take all the chocolate and cookies you wanted from Mr. Kern's candy store?" I said sharply.

"Oh, no, I wouldn't do such a thing." Rita was genuinely shocked. "That would be stealing, wouldn't it?"

"Honest, Thomas, we didn't mean to do it," Fatso Paul added hastily.

"Skip it," said Thomas.

"Cheer up, Rita," said Marianne, "I'll give you something for your little sisters."

"Really?"

"There's plenty left in the larder." Marianne ran back into the kitchen.

"What's going on in Old Square?" I asked.

"It's still the same," Karl reported. "They are all crazy."

"They shot at me with arrows," complained Bob Pell.

"Oscar and a bunch of Pirates are in the Red Kettle Inn, bowling," Karl continued. "They are walking all over the bowling alleys with their shoes on, which is strictly forbidden."

"Some kids are dancing in the ballroom; Minnie Cobb is playing the piano," Bob Pell added.

"I saw a lot of girls in Mrs. Diggin's Dress Shop," said Rita. "They are trying on all the hats and dresses."

"This will end badly," I threw in.

"Just imagine," grunted Fatso Paul. "Lots of kids throw the cakes they don't like into the gutter." He looked horrified.

Marianne returned with a basket and gave it to Rita. "Here, Rita. There are liverwurst sandwiches, milk, and apples for Lotti and Lisa."

"Thank you, Marianne. Thanks a lot," said Rita. "I'd better hurry now."

But Thomas held her back. "You can't go alone; it's dangerous."

"Why?" asked Rita, bewildered. "I live near the station plaza—that's far away from Old Square and Main Street where all the kids are."

"I still don't like it," said Thomas. "You may run into a few stray Pirates, and they'll want to know where you got the food."

"I won't tell," Rita said heroically.

"That's what you say now," Thomas continued, "but they may threaten you or take the basket away from you. No, we'll all go. There are five of us boys now, so a few Pirates aren't likely to attack us."

"Six," said Mark. "I'll fight, too."

"No, you won't," Thomas said angrily.

"But I will fight," Marianne said, and her eyes sparkled belligerently.

"Are you kidding?" I said. "You keep out of all fights." I was her cousin and felt responsible for her.

"Don't give yourself airs." She glared at me.

"OK, OK, cut it out," said Thomas, grinning. "No family quarrels, please. Let's get going."

"Of course we'll have to take Rita home," I said, "but what happens, Thomas, if some Pirates see us and run to get Oscar and his whole gang?"

Thomas scratched his head for a while. "I tell you what we'll do," he said finally. "We'll stay at Rita's until it is pitch dark. Fortunately, there will be no streetlights on in Timpetill tonight, as you know." He grinned again.

I had to admit it, Thomas was smart. He was a born leader. I was glad that he was on our side.

We left. This time we made sure that Marianne didn't forget her key. We hurried through several streets and alleys without meeting a soul, but when we turned the corner into Station Street, we almost stumbled over Otto Hoffman and his sister Karen. They were sitting dejectedly on the stoop in front of their house. We stopped short and stared at them. They were Pirates.

Both of them jumped up. "Thomas," cried Otto. "Boy, am I happy to see you."

Thomas was taken aback. "Why?" he said. "What are you so happy about?"

"We can't get into our house; we lost the key."

"That's tough luck," Thomas said bitingly. "Why don't you go to Main Street and spend the night in one of Mr. Kroning's beds in his furniture store?"

"Please, Thomas, don't be sore at us anymore," Karen said, and plucked timidly at his sleeve.

"We're through with Oscar and this Pirate business, I swear," said Otto.

Thomas turned to me. "Professor, take a look at that door lock. Maybe you can open it."

"Sorry," I said, "this is one of those newfangled safety locks. It's foolproof." It was true; my piece of wire was useless here.

"How awful!" wailed Karen. "We'll have to sleep out-of-doors. I'll be scared to death." Her eyes filled with tears.

"Pipe down," said Thomas. "Come along with us. We'll figure out later what to do with you for the night."

Otto and Karen cheered up considerably. "Thank you, Thomas," they both said.

We moved on, and Otto told us that a number of children were regretting already what they had done but kept quiet for fear of Oscar.

"They are cowards," said Marianne.

"Oscar was furious this morning, Thomas," Otto continued, "when the Pirates couldn't catch you in front of Town Hall. But Oscar has sworn that he will get even with you yet."

"Thomas is already shaking in his boots," I said with a sneer.

All of a sudden, Thomas stood still and listened intently. "Why is it so quiet at Old Square?" he asked.

"Because they all left a little while ago," Otto said.

"Where did they go?" I asked, alarmed. I looked around, but the street was empty.

"They went out to Hunchback Hill," said Otto. "We didn't join them—we'd had enough. They want to climb up to the ruins of the old castle and play knights and robber barons."

We breathed more easily. Hunchback Hill is out of town to the south, and we were going north.

"Oscar is the biggest robber baron there ever was," said Mark. We laughed, and Mark was flattered.

When we reached Rita's house, Lotti and Lisa ran across the lawn toward us.

"I have milk and sandwiches for you," said Rita.

"Oh, goody!" they exclaimed, clapping their hands.

"After they've eaten, you had better put them to bed," said Thomas.

"I'll help you, Rita," said Marianne. They took the little girls inside, and we sat down on the lawn. The sun was low on the horizon and had disappeared behind a bank of menacing clouds. It was sultry, as though a thunderstorm was brewing. We could hear Marianne and Rita bustling about the house, but there was complete silence in all the neighboring houses. We were lost in thought. It was nighttime and our parents still weren't back. Were they really that mad at us?

"Kids," Thomas said, "I just had a brainstorm."

We looked at him expectantly.

"How late is it, Professor?"

"Is that your brainstorm?" I asked.

"Quick, how late is it?"

"Take it easy," I said, and looked at my wrist-watch. I'm proud of my watch. It has a luminous dial, and I can read the time even in the dark. My Aunt Betty, who lives in America, sent it to me for Christmas. "It's exactly ten minutes to seven," I said.

"Then we can just make it," said Thomas cheer-fully. "We're not far from the station. The train from Kollersburg arrives at seven o'clock. And you know what, maybe our parents are on it."

We jumped in excitement.

"That would be lovely," Karen exclaimed.

"Marianne, Rita," Thomas yelled. "We're in a hurry. Let's go."

Marianne stuck her head out of a window. "Don't rush us, please," she yelled back, and slammed the window shut. But after a minute, both girls stepped out of the house, locked the door carefully, and joined us.

We walked hurriedly in single file between the trolley tracks toward the station plaza.

Our town is small, just a tiny spot on the map. Most people don't even know about us, but oddly enough, we have an electric streetcar. There is only one line, Line Number 1, and it runs between the station and Old Square. There are eleven stops. Whenever I take it, I stand up front with the motorman to see how he works the controls and pretend I am driving it myself. Of course, the streetcar was not running today because we had no electricity.

When we reached the station, the train was just pulling in. We leaped up to the platform and stopped. There was only one passenger coach, and no one got off. The conductor was standing near an open door, and the engineer was leaning out of his cab. They both were waiting for Mr. Werner, the stationmaster, to give them the signal.

The conductor saw us. "Hey, kids," he called, "where is Mr. Werner?"

"Mr. Werner?" said Thomas.

"Are you dumb?" snorted the conductor. "Yes, Mr. Werner, the stationmaster. Where is he?"

"Mr. Werner is—" Thomas said hesitatingly. "Mr. Werner is—he is in the forest."

"In the forest? What is he doing in the forest? He has to give us the signal to pull out."

I saw Thomas was in trouble. "Mr. Werner is picking mushrooms," I said quickly. It was a lie, but what else could I say? We couldn't tell the conductor that our parents had taken off because they were fed up with us; he would have thought we were kidding him. He didn't seem to be in a good mood, anyway.

But unexpectedly, he roared with laughter. "He's picking mushrooms! That's a good one. Well, if he loves mushrooms so much, we'll just have to get going without him this time." The engineer laughed, too.

"Excuse me, Mr. Conductor," Thomas said. "Did many people get on the train when it left for Kollersburg this morning?"

"None," the conductor said. "Why do you want to know?"

"Oh, I'm just curious," murmured Thomas.

The conductor blew his whistle. The locomotive hissed and emitted puffs of steam, and with a jerk the train started up. The conductor swung himself onto the steps of the moving coach and waved at us, still chuckling. The train rumbled across the bridge over Timpe Creek and soon disappeared into the tunnel.

"Our parents didn't come." Rita sighed. She was close to tears again.

"One thing is clear," Thomas said thoughtfully. "They didn't take the train to Kollersburg this morning. This means they must be in the forest. I'm baffled. It's getting dark already; they would be crazy to spend the night in the forest."

"My mother certainly wouldn't do it," Karen said. "She's scared to death of wild animals. She's even frightened of a deer or a rabbit."

"My father never misses reading the newspaper in the evening," said Fatso Paul.

"And my grandfather always feeds our parrot," said Bob Pell.

Downhearted though we were, this made us laugh.

"It looks as though you'll be feeding the parrot tonight," I said.

"Look, there's something on the platform," said Karl Benz.

At the end of the platform stood a dozen or so large tin milk cans. We ran over to them.

"It's the milk for Mrs. Sandrock," Otto Hoffman said. "The train brings it every day."

Mrs. Sandrock owns the dairy on Old Square. We counted the cans; there were fifteen. Thomas took the lid off one and peered inside. It was full of milk.

"Oh, boy!" said Fatso Paul. "May I have a sip?"

"No," said Thomas.

"What'll we do with it?" I asked.

Thomas scratched his head. "Somehow we must find a way to get it into town. Mrs. Sandrock has a cool-room. Otherwise, the milk will be sour by tomorrow."

"I like sour milk, too," said Fatso.

8

<hr/>

When a Horse Has a Cough

We stood around on the platform wondering how we could get the milk cans into town. They were so heavy that we could hardly lift them. And we hadn't much time left; huge, dark thunderclouds covered half the sky. We didn't know what to do.

"Couldn't we put the milk into milk bottles?" suggested Fatso Paul.

"And where do we get so many bottles?" asked Thomas.

"Why, everybody has a few milk bottles at home."

"Nuts," I said. "It would take us a million years."

"I know," said Otto Hoffman. "We can roll the milk cans to Old Square."

We greeted this stupid idea with icy silence.

"Mr. Wollinger has a horse and carriage," said Karl Benz.

"Bravo, Karl!" exclaimed Thomas, and slapped him on the shoulder. "That would solve our problem."

"But what about the Pirates?" asked Rita.

"Didn't you hear?" I said. "They all went to Hunchback Hill."

"We're lucky," Thomas said. "They can't be back for at least an hour. Let's hurry." He told Otto and Bob to stay at the station. He wanted them to watch the milk cans till we came back.

The Wollingers live on River Street right behind the station, so we didn't have far to go. The stables are behind the house in a courtyard. Thomas knocked at the front door of the main building, but nobody opened it.

"Gosh," I said, "we are nitwits. Max and Albert aren't home; they are with the others on Hunchback Hill."

"But I heard a noise behind the door," Marianne said.

Thomas knocked again.

"Yes? Who is it?" asked Max Wollinger.

"Me," said Thomas.

"Who is me?"

"Me, Thomas Wank. Open at once."

"Why?" Max's voice sounded frightened.

"Because of the milk."

"We have no milk."

"But we do have milk," Thomas yelled. "Open the door at once."

The door opened a crack. Thomas put his weight against it, and we all squeezed into the house. Max retreated and spread out his arms to protect his younger brother Albert. Maybe they thought we wanted to get even with them; they had been among the first to pounce on us in Old Square.

"Don't be silly," I said. "We won't eat you. We don't attack people in their houses. We're glad you're at home because we need the horse and carriage."

"What for?" asked Max.

"It's an emergency," I explained. "The train brought the milk, and the milk will turn sour if we don't get it to Mrs. Sandrock's cool-room as fast as possible."

"Sure, sure," said Max. He was breathing much easier. "You can have the carriage but not the horse."

"Why not?" asked Thomas.

"Hans is sick."

"Who's Hans?" asked Marianne.

"The horse," Max replied.

"What's the matter with him?" she asked anxiously.

"He has a cough."

"Take us to the stables," said Thomas, looking suspicious.

Max and Albert led us across the courtyard to the stables, and we went in. Near the entrance stood a victoria, an open one-horse carriage. In a corner, to the right, we saw Hans standing in front of a hay-filled manger. But he wasn't eating. His head hung low, and he didn't even turn it as we came in.

Marianne was worried. She stepped toward Hans, but Thomas pulled her back.

"Never approach a horse from the rear," he said. "It might get frightened and kick you. Always from the side, Marianne. Didn't you know that?"

"I've never had a horse," Marianne said, a bit edgy. Nevertheless, she kept at a respectful distance from the horse's hindquarters and approached him from the side. She wanted to stroke him but hesitated. "Does he bite, Max?" she asked.

"No, he is very gentle."

Marianne laid her hand on Hans's neck. "He feels hot," she said.

"He must be very sick not to eat," said Fatso Paul.

"Perhaps he has a sore throat," Mark suggested.

"He gets a cough once in a while," said Max. "Father just lets him stay in the stable for a couple of days until he gets well again."

"He ought to have a blanket around his neck," remarked Rita.

"That would do no harm," I said.

We had Max give us a horse blanket, and we

wrapped it around Hans's neck. Then we fastened a rope around the blanket so that it wouldn't fall off.

"What bad luck that the horse is sick," said Thomas.

"Maybe he could just make it to the square after all," said Karl Benz.

Marianne was up in arms. "How can you suggest such a thing? Shame on you! I would never let a sick horse work."

"Why don't we pull the carriage ourselves?" I said.

"A brilliant idea, Professor," Thomas exclaimed. "I'm an idiot; I should have thought of that myself. With Max and Albert, there are twelve of us. It'll be a cinch."

"I'm not a horse," Paul growled.

"But you would like to drink the milk, wouldn't you?" scoffed Marianne.

"Don't get fresh," Paul shouted.

"You're lazy, that's all," Marianne shouted back.

"Cut it out, will you?" Thomas intervened. "We have to stick together. Don't forget it."

We backed the carriage across the courtyard and through the gate and then pushed and pulled it over to the station platform. Robert and Otto were still sitting beside the milk cans, dangling their legs. They were both flabbergasted when they saw us.

"Where's the horse?" asked Robert.

"We're the horse," Fatso Paul grumbled.

"The horse is sick," said Thomas. "Come on, get going. We have to get the cans into the carriage."

That was easier said than done; they were heavy and slippery. One crashed to the pavement, the lid flew off, and all the milk gushed into the gutter.

"Help! The milk!" cried Fatso Paul. He knelt down and started to lap it up.

"Have you gone mad?" Thomas snapped at him. "Stop that immediately. Give us a hand."

Fortunately, the accident with the milk can wasn't too bad. We had no room for all the cans in the carriage, anyway. Seven fitted into the rear, and we could put only three on the coach box. We had to abandon the rest.

After much heaving, lifting, and groaning, the job was finally done.

"OK," panted Thomas, breathing heavily. "Now listen. Otto, Max, Robert, Karl, Professor, and I, we'll get into the shafts and pull. Paul, Mark, Albert, and the girls will push from behind." We did as he told us, but after a few feet of pulling and pushing, Thomas stopped us. "Hold it," he said. "I forgot something important."

"What?" we asked.

"Somebody has to sit on the coachman's box."

"But why?" I protested. "This isn't a joyride. The carriage with all the milk cans is heavy enough without somebody's sitting on the coachman's box."

"I know," said Thomas, "but it can't be helped. Some stretches on Station Street go steeply downhill. Somebody has to apply the brakes or else the carriage will run us down like a steamroller."

"You're right, Thomas," I admitted.

The brake business started an uproar. Almost all the kids wanted to sit on the coachman's box.

Fatso Paul shouted the loudest. "I'm a wonderful brakeman—I'm a wonderful brakeman!"

I didn't join them; I was one of the oldest and strongest and was needed on the shafts. "Let Rita sit on the coachman's box," I said. "She's the smallest and lightest."

Thomas was against it. "No," he said. "Rita isn't strong enough to work the brake. I'm for Marianne; she is light but strong."

Marianne beamed and smiled at him. "Thank you, Thomas," she said.

Now Karen was angry. "Marianne is no stronger than I am." But Marianne had already climbed onto the coachman's seat. It wasn't too comfortable up there because she had to dangle her legs over the milk cans, but she didn't seem to mind. She took the whip, cracked it, and called, "Giddap!"

"Stop cracking the whip," snapped Fatso Paul.

We started once more. In the beginning, our job wasn't too hard. We could use the trolley tracks to Old Square because they were the same width as the wheels of the carriage, and as long as the ground was level, we got on smoothly.

Marianne was cracking the whip again, just for the fun of it, and singing at the same time, "Oh, the old gray mare, she ain't what she used to be . . ."

In Station Street we saw small groups of children creeping home. When we called to them to help us, they ran off. They looked afraid. I guess it was the threatening thunderstorm. We didn't feel too cheerful either. Even Marianne had stopped singing. The weather was really nasty now. The sky was as black as coal, heat lightning flashed on the horizon, and we could hear the rumble of distant thunder. And, of course, there were no streetlights on and no light shone from the houses.

We were going downhill. Marianne applied the brakes with all her might, and we took it easy. But soon after, the street began to climb, and we had to push and pull like mad. Just before the top of the hill, we got stuck; we couldn't move the carriage one inch further. It even started to roll backwards, and if Marianne hadn't had the presence of mind to

apply the brakes again, everything would have been
lost. Then Marianne jumped down from her seat to
help push, but it was no use. With the brakes on,
the carriage wouldn't budge.

"We're beaten!" I groaned.

"We need help," Thomas snorted, and looked
around.

Kurt and Irma Kroeger, the postman's children,
and Ernest Werner, the son of the stationmaster,
were standing on the sidewalk. They were staring
at us dumfounded.

"Don't stand there like idiots," Thomas yelled
at them. "Come on and pitch in. We have to bring
in the milk."

The three didn't stir.

"You're a bunch of sissies," Marianne cried.

That did it. They came to life and rushed over to us. Marianne hurried back onto the coachman's box to release the brakes, and with the help of Kurt, Irma, and Ernest, who were strong kids, we finally made the top of the hill. We paused to catch our breath.

Ernest told us that most of the children had left Hunchback Hill for home because of the threatening storm and the growing darkness. Only Oscar and a dozen or so of his Pirates boasted they would stick it out in the ruins of the castle.

"I hope they get drenched," said Marianne.

Thomas looked up at the sky. "We'd better hurry up or *we* will get drenched," he said.

We were on a level stretch now and managed the sharp curve that brought us into Main Street without much trouble. From here on, the trolley tracks run downhill almost all the way to Old Square, except for the last three blocks. By that time, we had gained so much speed that the carriage rolled up the incline under its own momentum. The tracks came to an end at Old Square, and we had to maneuver the carriage over the bumpy cobblestone pavement to Mrs. Sandrock's dairy. This was a difficult job.

The square was in a state of wild disorder; hundreds of toys were scattered everywhere, just as the children had left them. Scooters, roller skates, football helmets, bicycles, and dolls were strewn about, and the whole place was littered with empty candy boxes, loose Indian feathers, picture books, and scraps of paper. We were appalled.

"Wow!" I exclaimed. "This looks worse than our town dump. They sure made a mess here."

"They're vandals," hissed Marianne.

"We'll have to clean up," said Thomas, "as soon as we are through with the milk."

"Wait a minute," I said. "Are you serious? Why should we do it?"

"That's the Pirates' business," said Mark.

"Don't kid yourselves," said Thomas. "They'll do nothing. But if our parents should come back tonight and see this, they would turn straight around and leave us for good."

I didn't know what to say.

"Of course we'll clean up," said Marianne. "Or do you want to be sent to reform school?"

"Don't exaggerate," I mumbled.

Mark was wide-eyed and didn't move. The idea that our parents might never come back seemed to have paralyzed him. The other children didn't dare to speak up because they had taken part in the plundering.

"All right, all right, Thomas," I grunted, "we'll clean up, but we won't get any medals for it."

"Oh, shut up," said Thomas. We were all a bit edgy now. We'd had a tough and exciting day and nothing to eat since our peanut butter sandwiches at Marianne's.

After we had dragged the milk cans into Mrs. Sandrock's cool-room, we went right to work on Old Square. But it had grown so dark that we couldn't see much.

"We need flashlights," I said. "Wait for me. I know where to get some." I made my way through all the debris into Main Street and entered Nisser's Motorbike Shop. Otto, Karl, and Bob joined me a short time later, and after much fumbling around in the dark, we found flashlights on a shelf near the window. We took fifteen back to Old Square and distributed them. Then we all spread out. Thomas, Kurt, and I hauled the big telescope back to Mr. Potz's store; the other boys returned the toys to the shops where they belonged, and the girls picked up the litter and stuffed it into garbage cans in the back-yards. We darted about like gremlins, the beams of our flashlights flickering eerily over the cobblestones and the walls of the houses.

We had almost finished the cleanup job when the thunderstorm finally caught up with us. Blinding flashes of lightning illuminated the entire sky; thunderclap followed thunderclap, and a cloudburst hit us like a deluge.

We fled into the covered alleyway of the dairy.

"Oh, gosh! Father's carriage!" Max Wollinger cried, horrified. The carriage stood in the rain with its top down.

"Quick," shouted Thomas above the storm, "we have to bring it in here."

We pushed and pulled the carriage into the alleyway and slammed the gate shut. The carriage was saved, but we were not. There was now no room in the alleyway for us. We stood tightly squeezed together under the awning of the dairy, and the wind blew the rain against us. We were soaking wet in no time.

"Let's run home," Rita wailed.

"No one must go home in this storm," said Thomas. "It's too dangerous."

"But it's awful here," complained Karen Hoffman. "The water is pouring down my back."

"We must get to the nearest shelter," said Thomas, and looked around. He tried the door of the dairy, but it was locked.

"Let's run to the cool-room in the rear," said Karl Benz.

"You're nuts," snorted Bob. "We'll freeze to death in there."

"I've got it!" I cried. "The Red Kettle Inn! It's only one block from here on the next corner."

"Hurrah!" yelled the others. We raced down the sidewalk, the girls laughing and squealing as we jumped over the puddles, and burst through the entrance of the inn right into the dining room.

9

A Fellow Has to Eat

"I'm freezing," said Rita Strauss, sneezing violently. It was cold inside the inn. We sat huddled on tables and chairs, waiting for the storm to abate. Everybody was dripping. The feeling of wet socks in our soaking shoes was particularly nasty. I placed several of the flashlights on the floor. Their beams of light reflected against the white ceiling, so that we did not have to sit in the dark.

Marianne pushed back her drenched hair and remarked, "I hope we won't catch pneumonia."

"It would be wonderful to have some heat." Fatso Paul sighed.

"They have central heating here," I said. Then my eye fell on a fireplace in the opposite wall. I jumped up. "Kids, there's a fireplace. We can make a fire and dry our clothes."

"Great!" exclaimed the others gleefully.

"Wait," I said. "First, let's see whether it works."

A huge copper kettle was hanging in the middle of the fireplace, but it was so shiny that it looked as if it had never been used.

"I hope there is a real chimney."

"We'll soon find out," said Robert Pell. He crawled into the fireplace and pulled himself up until only his spindly legs showed. When he reappeared, his face was black with soot.

"If this isn't a real chimney, I'll eat my hat," he reported. We all were laughing because he looked like a chimney sweep.

"As long as we have a fireplace, let's get some wood," said Thomas cheerfully.

Thomas, Otto, Karl, and I all grabbed flashlights and immediately began to search for wood. There was none inside, so we went out into the courtyard. It was still raining heavily. In one corner stood a half-open shed containing a huge woodpile. We loaded up with as many logs as we could carry and returned to the inn. Thomas folded up old papers for kindling, placed them in the fireplace, and piled the logs expertly over them.

"Now all we need is a match," he said, straightening up.

Once more we set out on a search but returned empty-handed.

"Not a match in the place," I said.

"Our parents must have taken all the matches with them," said Kurt Kroeger. "I couldn't find any at home, either."

No one else had any.

"That was very foresighted of our parents," said Thomas, "but somehow we must get dried out." He looked at me challengingly. "Professor, invent some way to make fire quick!"

"It's been taken care of already," I said smugly, and pulled an old banged-up lighter out of my pocket. I had found it in a ditch the week before. "It's a good lighter," I added. "It's out of fuel, but I'm sure we can find some here."

"Look in the kitchen first," Thomas said.

We ran into the kitchen and looked through all the drawers and shelves. Karen found a little bottle filled with a colorless liquid. "It smells like lighter fluid," she said triumphantly.

It really was lighter fluid. I filled the lighter and flipped the wheel, but nothing happened.

"Hm," I said, perplexed. "Something's wrong here. It doesn't seem to work."

Thomas grabbed the lighter and turned the wheel furiously, but he had no luck either. "Professor," he said, "you're an idiot. This lighter doesn't have a flint."

"Oh," I said, abashed. "I've never used it." I

searched desperately all over the kitchen to find something with which to light the fire. After being called an idiot, I had to show Thomas.

In a corner stood a large grindstone, the kind scissor-grinders use. "Just wait. I'll make sparks," I announced, and picked up a big kitchen knife. I strode over to the grindstone, cranked it, and pressed the knife against it. Sparks flew like fireworks. "Thomas, bring the lighter," I commanded.

Thomas knew at once what I had in mind. He held the lighter near the grindstone. A few sparks hit the wick, which quickly caught fire.

"Bravo, Professor," said Thomas.

"Michael is wonderful!" the girls called.

I felt pretty proud. "One shouldn't throw in the towel right away," I said offhandedly.

Thomas moved cautiously into the dining room, taking care not to let the flame go out. Then he lit the paper in the fireplace, and in no time a great fire was roaring and blazing. We gathered around the fireplace and took off our shoes and socks to hang near the fire to dry.

Soon we felt warm and snug. Every so often, Thomas put a few more logs on the fire. We would have been completely happy if our stomachs hadn't started to rumble with hunger.

"I'm dying of hunger," moaned Fatso Paul finally. His voice sounded as though it came from the grave.

"Me, too! Me, too!" several others complained. "We haven't even had breakfast."

"Quiet, everybody!" said Thomas. "Let me think where we might find something to eat."

"How stupid can you be or are you blind?" I asked.

"What do you mean?" demanded Thomas.

"I mean we needn't look very far. This happens to be an inn."

Thomas was struck dumb, and I smiled. Now I had paid him back for his "idiot."

Fatso Paul jumped up eagerly. "Oh, boy! Now we can eat whatever we want!"

"Not so fast," said Thomas. "We'll take only what we really need. We'll make a note of everything on a piece of paper, and everyone will sign his name. We'll leave the note here."

"That's known as requisitioning," I said importantly.

"I don't care what you call it," Thomas continued. "Our parents will have to pay for the food when they get back. There's nothing we can do about it. After all, we can't be expected to eat shoe leather."

We all agreed with him and, clutching flashlights, ran barefoot across the kitchen to the larder.

It was full of provisions. Hams and sausages hung from the ceiling, and on the shelves lay cheeses as big as wheels. There were baskets of eggs, jars of preserves, long loaves of bread, and trays heaped with doughnuts. Barrels of butter, sacks of potatoes, baskets of vegetables, crates of bananas, and many other delicacies were spread before our hungry eyes. Fatso Paul wanted to eat everything at once. We laughed at him. It would have taken us a week to eat it all.

"We mustn't make any unnecessary expenses for our parents," said Thomas. He had been taught to be thrifty. "We will take some bread and spread it with butter, and everyone will get a piece of cheese."

We protested violently. "We're not Spartans," I said.

"Hot soup would be best," said Marianne. "My father says people should always eat something hot at least once a day. He studied medicine," she added.

Everyone agreed about soup.

"How about some noodle soup?" said Rita.

"No, cream of spinach," said Ernest Werner.

"Oh, no, not that!" some of them cried in disgust.

"I'm all for beef broth, with chunks of meat in it," ventured Fatso Paul, gesticulating wildly. "And after that, we could have hot dogs or ham with spaghetti or sauerkraut. Then for dessert, we could have nut cake with whipped cream and top it all off with a chocolate sundae."

"Have you gone off your rocker?" shouted Thomas. "You have crazy ideas! But I'm all for hot soup," he went on more calmly. "We'll peel potatoes and onions, boil them, and throw in some bouillon cubes. Then everyone will get a slice of bread and butter. That's plenty."

"Not for me," grumbled Fatso Paul.

We put what we needed into a basket. I tore a sheet of paper out of my notebook and carefully made a complete list of everything we had taken. Then I put my signature under it, and the other children also carefully scribbled their names.

There was no glue, so we pasted the list on the door by dipping the corner of the sheet in honey.

"Where do we cook the soup?" asked Marianne.

"On the stove, of course," said Kurt Kroeger with a mocking grin.

"Very clever," said Marianne haughtily, screwing up her face, "but the stove happens to be electric, and there is no electricity."

"How stupid can we be?" I groaned.

"Well, that settles the soup," said Karl Benz.

"Why don't we just open up some cans?" said

Fatso Paul, filled with fresh hope. "There is smoked salmon, sardines, canned meat, herring in wine sauce, pickled pigs' knuckles."

"Oh, cut it out, boy! You're a pig yourself," said Robert Pell in disgust.

"And what do you think you are?" replied Fatso Paul furiously.

Thomas interrupted them. "Don't fight, or you won't get anything at all. We'll go without soup. We'll eat bread and butter, and everyone can have a banana."

"But that isn't hot," Marianne insisted. She was stubborn.

"We could toast the bread in the fireplace," Irma Kroeger suggested.

"Boy!" I exclaimed. "I've got it! Irma's given me an idea. There's a big copper kettle hanging in the fireplace. Why don't we make our soup in the kettle over the fire?"

"Great!" the children shouted jubilantly. A few of them ran out of the kitchen and came back with the kettle. It was as shiny inside as it was outside. Marianne took it to the sink and turned on the faucet. No water came out.

"Where's the water?" she said indignantly, her eyes flashing.

"The water has been turned off," I said.

"Why didn't you say so before?"

"Because I forgot," I confessed.

Marianne looked at me reproachfully.

"Our parents are making it pretty tough for us," said Ernest Werner bitterly.

"You're all terribly dense," said Thomas. "Can't you see it's raining?"

"So what?" we asked stupidly.

"The rain barrel is full—we have all the water we need."

We quickly filled the kettle and brought it back into the inn. The girls started to peel potatoes and onions. Thomas and I hung the kettle on the hook over the fireplace. Marianne and Rita threw in what they had prepared, and Karen had the happy idea of adding a handful of salt. After a while, Marianne, Rita, Karen, and Irma began to stir the brew with a huge wooden spoon that they had found in the kitchen.

"Too many cooks spoil the broth," muttered Fatso Paul with concern.

Finally, Marianne tasted the soup.

"How does it taste?" we all asked eagerly.

"Like rainwater," she said meekly.

10

Who's Afraid of Ghosts?

It was midnight before Marianne, Thomas, Mark, and I were finally able to go home. We had tidied everything up and washed the kettle, plates, and spoons. Then Thomas insisted that we wait until the fire in the fireplace went out.

"One can't be too careful with fire," he said.

You can always tell a good Boy Scout, I thought wryly.

The other children had left immediately after eating their soup and bread. They were ready to collapse with exhaustion and would have been no help to us. Otto Hoffman and his sister Karen, who had lost the key to their apartment, had to look for another place to sleep. Otto went home with Ernest Werner, and Karen with Rita.

When the four of us at last emerged into Old Square, the church clock was just striking twelve. The rain had stopped, and the moon and a few stars shone between gaps in the clouds. The puddles in front of the Town Hall reflected the moonlight.

"It's midnight," I said, "the witching hour." I almost never stay up that late. Ten o'clock is my usual bedtime because I have to get up at seven in the morning to go to school.

"Good-bye," Marianne murmured. "I'll run home."

"Wait, we'll go with you," said Thomas.

"Why, I'm not afraid." She laughed, but she sounded a bit uneasy.

"Let's play it safe," said Thomas. "There might still be some Pirates roaming around. I'm sure they know by now that you're on our side. Oscar's spies are everywhere."

"If they do anything to me, I'll punch them in the nose," Marianne said, her eyes flashing. But she no longer objected to our taking her home.

Her feet were sore, and she linked arms with Thomas and me. Mark Himmel trailed along behind us, his head drooping. "Aren't you afraid to be alone at night?" he asked.

"Heavens, no," said Marianne.

"Not even of ghosts?"

"Pooh, who says there are ghosts?" scoffed Marianne.

"I do," he muttered.

"They're only in your head," Thomas sneered.

Mark fell silent.

We had turned the corner of the church and were just going past the cemetery fence when Mark stopped, petrified. "Oh, no!" he gasped.

"What's the matter?" I asked, startled.

"L—l—*look*," Mark breathed, his face as white as a sheet.

We all looked and froze with fright. Behind one of the tombstones there emerged a yellow shriveled head. It seemed to nod at us. Then it vanished.

"How horrible!" Marianne groaned, her eyes wide with horror.

I'm no scaredy-cat, but I felt the goose pimples down my back. Again the head popped up. This

time it wavered from side to side. Thomas was startled, too. Then suddenly he broke into gales of laughter.

"Kids, don't panic. It's nothing but one of the balloons that drifted over from Old Square. It got caught behind a tombstone."

"Boy," I croaked, "that did look spooky."

We sighed with relief, but we had hardly taken three steps when we heard a long, wailing howl. Again we froze with terror. Marianne clutched our arms. "Help! What can that be?"

The howling changed to a whine, which finally became a human sob.

"Oh, oh, oh!"

Thomas tore himself free and ran across to the other side of Church Street. A ground-floor window was open in one of the houses. He peered into it. "So it's you, Fritz," he exclaimed. "Stop bawling and pull yourself together."

We walked over and looked into the room. The pale moonlight was pouring into the bedroom. On the bed sat Fritz Arnfeld, one of the Pirates.

"Why are you blubbering?" Thomas snapped.

"A ghost," he whimpered, pointing toward the cemetery.

"Nonsense," said Thomas. "That's only a balloon. It serves you right. You shouldn't have stolen them in the first place." He pushed down the window and slammed the outside shutters tight. Marianne and I rocked with laughter, and Thomas joined in. It was a nervous reaction to the scare we had just had. We were still laughing when we got to Marianne's house, but Mark remained glum.

"Good night," Marianne said, giggling.

"Are you sure you have your key?" I inquired with a grin.

"Oh, yes," she said. "Many thanks for escorting me. To tell the truth, I'm glad that I didn't have to walk alone," she said bashfully.

"Well, we know the right thing to do," Thomas replied smugly.

Marianne ran into the house and slammed the front door behind her. She pushed her nose against one of the windowpanes, waved at us, and vanished quick as a squirrel.

"Mark, now you run home, too," said Thomas.

Mark lived nearby, in Corner Street. He hesitated. Suddenly he turned around, put his head against a wall, and began to cry. Thomas and I were embarrassed. Nobody likes to see boys cry. After all, Mark was thirteen years old. Thomas and I exchanged an unhappy look. I took off my glasses, cleaned them with deliberation, and put them on again.

"Hm," I growled at last, clearing my throat. "What's the matter, Mark?"

"I'm afraid that I won't ever see my mother again," he mumbled through his sobs.

"Take it easy," said Thomas. "Your mother will be back tomorrow."

Mark turned around and looked at him searchingly. "Do you really think so?"

"I'm sure of it," said Thomas. "Come on, you can sleep at my house tonight." He took Mark's arm and walked off with him in the direction of Hill Street.

It was high time for me to go home, too. Yet I made a detour around the cemetery, preferring the longer walk through the winding mews to Main Street, and then to Old Square. When I reached home, I tried to turn my flashlight on in the hall. The batteries were dead, so I had to climb the stairs in the dark. Being all alone in the house gave me an eerie feeling. The stairs creaked protestingly under my weight, a door squeaked, and a window rattled in the kitchen. It sounded like a crocodile gnashing its teeth. I was glad when I at last reached my room. I locked the door—something I ordinarily never do. I undressed quickly and jumped into bed and was just about to settle down when a bloodcurdling howl came from outside the window. I sat bolt upright, my whole body shivering and shaking.

"Who's there?"

Then I remembered Peter, the cat. He liked to sit on the roof and glower at the neighbor's cat. The way they howl at each other is enough to make one's hair stand on end. I liked Peter, but at that moment I could have tied a rocket to his tail to send him scooting to the moon. "Nobody can possibly sleep with his infernal caterwauling and mewing," I said to myself—and fell asleep.

11

Fifteen Friends in Need

I was dreaming that I had fallen into a milk can as tall as a house and was swimming desperately to keep myself from drowning when somebody banged at my door. In a state of confusion, I shot upright in bed. "Who's there?" I called.

"It's me, Thomas."

I jumped out of bed, ran to the door, and unlocked it.

"Why did you lock the door?" asked Thomas. "Did you have the jitters last night, too?"

"I always lock the door," I lied brazenly.

"They're not here," said Thomas grimly.

"Who isn't here?" I asked absentmindedly. I was still trying to recover from my nightmare.

"Our parents, of course, you dope. Who else? They haven't come back."

"Oh, boy! What a mess! Where can they be?" I hastily dove into my clothes.

"On the North Pole or in the jungle, for all I know. Hurry up and get dressed. There's a lot to do," said Thomas.

"So early?" I looked out of the window. Dawn was just breaking, and the sun had not yet appeared on the horizon.

"We must beat the Pirates to it," Thomas continued. "They're still sleeping like logs. Mark, Marianne, and I have been up since five. We made sure to lock up all the stores properly."

"What, Marianne up so early?" I said in amazement.

Thomas grinned. "We had to wake her up because she had all the store keys. Don't you remember?"

"Where are the two of them now? Why didn't they come up?" I mumbled. I was rinsing my teeth with the last bit of water that happened to have been left in a glass.

"I sent them off to round up all our allies of yesterday. We'll meet in my father's workshop. So make it snappy, Professor."

"What do you want us to do?" I asked, as I hastily combed my hair.

"Distribute bulletins."

"Bulletins? Why bulletins?" I looked at him in bewilderment.

"We want to put a bulletin under the door of every house in Timpetill in which there are children. They'll all be completely starved."

"They can't eat bulletins," I said, still not catching on.

"Idiot, they're supposed to *read* them." Thomas was growing irritated. "Now hurry up and get ready. We'll need about three hundred bulletins."

"What are you going to say?"

" 'Come to Old Square. There will be milk, doughnuts, and bananas.' Getting the milk from the station yesterday is a break for us today. We'll get the doughnuts and bananas at the Red Kettle Inn."

"Your plan stinks," I said.

"Why?"

"Did you stop to think how long it would take us to write three hundred bulletins? Each of us would have to write at least twenty. And I happen to know about the miserable writing of some of the others. It would take them at least a quarter of an hour for each bulletin."

"Hmph," grunted Thomas, trying to figure out in his head what fifteen times twenty was. At last he had the answer. "Why, that would mean five hours," he said ruefully. "By that time the Pirates will be all over the place."

"Don't panic," I said. "We'll print the bulletins."

"How? What? Print? Where?"

"In Mr. Posner's printing shop. You can print three hundred bulletins in no time at all. Besides, type looks a hundred times more important than something in longhand. And do you know what? We won't print bulletins, we'll print large posters. We'll paste them on the walls all over town. You'll see, this will really do the trick."

"That's great, Professor, but do you know how to use a printing press?"

"Nothing to it," I said. "Mr. Posner often lets me help him."

"Well, let's go, then," Thomas said.

Just before we reached Hill Street, Marianne came running toward us. "What took you so long?" she scolded. "We've been sitting in the shop for ages between those smelly boots, waiting for you."

"We had something important to discuss," I said.

"Really? What?" she said suspiciously. She wore a pretty dress and looked neat and fresh and ladylike. Her hair was damp.

"Tell me, Marianne. By any chance did you wash?" I asked.

"Sure. I even took a shower. There!" She stuck her tongue out at me, which wasn't so ladylike.

"A shower? How did you manage that? There isn't any water."

"We have a rain barrel in our garden. I took a watering can, filled it, and poured it over myself in the tub."

"Hey, wait a minute." Thomas stood still. "Marianne just gave me a good idea. Let's fill a lot of watering cans and take them to Old Square. Then we'll make all the children wash themselves before we hand out any food."

"We'll also write in the bulletin that they must bring soap and towels," Marianne said excitedly.

"We aren't writing any bulletins. We're going to print them," I said.

"How divine!" Marianne glowed as though I had made her a lovely present.

All our friends of the previous day had gathered in the workshop. Rita Strauss had brought Lotti and Lisa along, as she didn't want to leave them at home alone. They were sitting on a stool, their arms around each other. The others crowded around noisily.

"We were beginning to think you'd forgotten us," said Karl Benz.

"We don't forget our friends," said Thomas.

"How many notes do we have to write?" Otto Hoffman asked nervously.

"None. We're going to print posters," said Thomas, and explained what we had in mind.

"Hurrah!" the children yelled in chorus. They were relieved that we didn't have to write. Most of them didn't even like to read, despite our teacher's constant reminder of the importance of knowing how to read and write. Without that, he insisted, one could not get anywhere in life. As a matter of fact, we would have been in a bad fix during this emergency if I hadn't remembered most of the things I had read.

"How are we going to make the posters stick?" asked Ernest Werner.

"There's lots of glue in our stationery store," I said. "We'll get it later. First let's print the posters."

We started on our way. Only Rita had to stay behind because Lotti and Lisa were too small to take along.

Mr. Posner's print shop is a small factory-like building on Main Street. We had the shopping bag with us with all the store keys, but none of them would fit, and the windows were bolted from inside. The lock was a new, burglar-proof one. We walked around the building and discovered a round ventilator in the back. It was just below the roof and difficult to reach.

"Mark, you'll have to squeeze through it. You're the only one who can make it," Thomas ordered.

The opening was about the size of the lid of a small garbage pail.

"I'll be glad to," said Mark gamely. "But how am I going to get up there? I can't fly."

"We'll make a ladder for you," said Thomas. "Bob Pell is tall. He can stand on my shoulders, and you can climb on top of both of us."

"That's fine," I said. "But what's he supposed to do after he's squeezed himself through the opening? Once inside the house, he won't be able to jump down from such a height. He might break a leg."

"What we need is a strong rope," Kurt Kroeger suggested. "We could hold it out here and then lower him with it inside the house."

That seemed like a sensible idea, and we went off to find a rope. We looked around but didn't see anything suitable and soon returned. Only Karl Benz, Max Wollinger, and Otto Hoffman stayed away a long time. They had strayed further off, into some of the backyards. When at last they turned up again, they were dragging a long garden hose behind them.

"Will this do?" called Karl Benz.

"Great," said Thomas. "It's even better than a rope."

Thomas leaned against the wall, and we hoisted Bob Pell onto his shoulders. Like a monkey, Mark scrambled on top of both. Feetfirst, he let himself through the vent hole, because he didn't want to land on his head. We handed him one end of the garden hose, which he grabbed with both hands, and then he slowly disappeared. We kept the hose taut, paying off a bit at a time until it became slack. Almost immediately a ground-floor window flew open, and Mark waved at us, grinning. "Nothing to it," he said, panting.

I was the first one through the window and at once busied myself with the type trays. We had no time to lose. The narrow arched windows of our church glowed with the crimson rays of the early morning sun.

While I was picking out the largest type faces I could find, Thomas dictated to Marianne what we wanted to print. She carefully wrote it down on a piece of paper, holding her head to one side and every once in a while running her tongue over her lips.

"How shall we sign it?" she asked.

"What do you mean?" asked Thomas.

"It should say who wrote it. Otherwise, all the children might think it's from our parents again."

"Put all our names on it," several boys cried excitedly. Everyone would have given an eyetooth to see his name in print.

"Out of the question. That would take much too long," I objected.

"You lazybones. It's still early," cried several of the children.

"Silence!" said Thomas. "No one is permitted to talk out of turn at a meeting. We will take a vote, but remember, one at a time. Max Wollinger, you start."

"With what?" Max said, completely perplexed.

"You should suggest what must come last on the poster."

"A period," said Max.

Thomas turned away from him in utter disgust.

"Ernest Werner, you have the floor."

"I—I—" he stammered. "What do you want me to say?"

"Who wrote the poster?"

"We did," said Ernest.

Thomas heaved a sigh.

"Paul Brandt," he called.

"Here." Fatso Paul jumped up. He had been dozing in a corner.

"What do you suggest?"

"Fried eggs with French fries." He thought we were talking about breakfast.

"Sign it 'Friends in Need,' " said Irma Kroeger.

Almost everybody agreed to this.

"How many 'Friends in Need' are we?" I said.

Except for the signature, all the type was set, and I had even remembered to allow for the spaces between each word. I wrapped string around each line of type, just as Mr. Posner did, to keep the type from falling out. Now all that was needed was the signature.

Thomas counted the children. "Marianne, Michael, Mark, Paul, Otto, Karen, Karl, Max, Albert, Bob, Kurt, Irma, and Ernest. Thirteen," he said.

"Oh, gosh, that's an unlucky number," wailed Bob Pell.

"You forgot yourself, Thomas," I said.

"Correct. So that means we are fourteen."

"No, fifteen," said Marianne. "We mustn't leave out Rita. She helped us bring the milk into town yesterday."

"All right, then. Fifteen," said Thomas.

I quickly set the signature, then transferred all the type onto an old-fashioned make-up galley. The others followed and watched me intently. I threw the switch for the motor, to start the press. Nothing happened. Again I had forgotten that we had no electricity.

"Professor, you goofed," said Thomas.

I stared at the machine, lost in thought.

"Perhaps it will run if you tickle it a bit," said Bob Pell.

"Couldn't we turn the big wheel on the side ourselves?" asked Thomas.

"Of course," I exclaimed hopefully. "Everybody lend a hand. It's hard to turn."

Thomas, Max Wollinger, and Karl Benz took hold of the spokes, and the wheel began to turn. So did the rollers.

"Good," I said. "Now we can print. It will be slow this way, but we'll just print a hundred. But first, I want to print a proof sheet."

I selected the largest sheet of paper I could find and placed it on the machine. Clamps pressed it against the type bed, and it disappeared beneath the rollers to emerge on the other side, where it automatically dropped on the delivery board. Marianne rushed up and grabbed the sheet.

"There's print on it," she exclaimed jubilantly.

We rushed to her side and looked at it with reverence. In my haste, I had made a few misspellings, but this did not bother us. We read the message:

CHILDREN OF TIMPETILL

Come to Old Skuare. There will be milk, down-uts, and bannanas. Bring cups or small dishes, but nothing brekable. Our parents hav not yet returned, but don't lose courage. We must stick together and maintain pease and order. Don't listen to Oscar and the Pirates. Also bring soap and toweles. We have water for washing and want to help you in the absense of our parents.

Fifteen Friends in Need

12

White Coal

Our poster was a great success. The children of Timpetill poured into Old Square from all directions. Armed with tin cups and dishes, they waited in long lines for their breakfast. Most of them brought along soap and towels.

Their cockiness of yesterday had vanished. After spending the night in dark houses, abandoned by parents, their spirits were dampened. They were also famished, but according to our plan, they were to wash before getting anything to eat. Karl Benz, Bob Pell, and Karen Hoffman stood beside the statue with the watering cans. Only after each child had washed his hands and face was he allowed to run across to Marianne, where again they lined up. We had poured some of Mrs. Sandrock's milk into bowls and pans, so the cans didn't weigh so much and could be brought to the square. Marianne poured the milk into a big ladle, and each person received only a ladleful, because we were afraid that there would not be enough. Fatso Paul kept an eye on the cans to prevent anyone from secretly taking an extra dip with his own cup. Max Wollinger and his brother Albert watched the line to make sure that nobody took a second turn. A few steps further on, near the corner of Church Street, doughnuts and bananas were piled on a board, propped on two crates. Rita Strauss and Irma Kroeger stood behind the make-shift counter, handing each child two doughnuts and one banana. Otto Hoffman, Ernest Werner, and Kurt Kroeger were keeping order there.

While all this was going on, Thomas, Mark, and I sat on the steps of the Town Hall. We put our heads together to plan what to do with the children after breakfast.

"We must think of something to keep them busy," said Thomas. "Otherwise, they'll start some mischief again."

"Let's make up a work schedule for them," I proposed. "We will write down everything so that we won't forget anything important."

Thomas nodded in agreement. Marianne had finished ladling out the milk and joined us on the steps.

"You lazybones," she said. "You're not doing a thing. I can hardly move my arm from all this ladling."

She looked hot, and she lifted her hair from her neck. The sun was shining, and it was getting warm. We were wondering why the Pirates had not yet shown up. We were afraid that they might suddenly descend on us. All the girl Pirates had come over to our side because they had finally had their fill of Oscar, but most of the boy Pirates were still sticking with him.

As the children finished eating, they began to cluster around us, and little by little the throng grew.

"Those posters were a great idea," said Herbert Brisk.

Thomas spotted Fritz Bollner in the crowd and signaled him to step up. "Say, Fritz, where's Oscar?"

"The Pirates have retreated to the park at Timpe Creek. I went along at first, but then I pulled out

to come over to your side. They tore down all the posters on their way to the park. 'We're going to beat up those Fifteen Friends in Need,' Oscar said."

"I hope they'll stay away for a while," I said. "What are they doing in the park, anyway?"

"They're playing on the merry-go-round and the slides, and they've taken the rowboats out of the boathouse to row on the pond."

"Aren't they starving, too?" asked Thomas.

"Not a bit," Fred Spitzer reported. He, too, had deserted the Pirates. "They picked a lot of apples and pears on Mr. Denk's farm. They even took eggs from his chicken house."

"It's a shame," Marianne said.

"Are we going to get something more to eat today?" Gustav Bosnick inquired.

"We can't keep eating doughnuts all the time," mumbled another boy.

"Since our parents left, I haven't had anything warm to eat," complained Harold Knoll. He was fat, like Paul Brandt.

"There's no way of cooking anything here," said Thomas.

"Why don't we go back to the Red Kettle Inn to cook?" said Marianne. "There would be room there for all the kids. They could sit on the benches at the tables."

"The kettle in the fireplace is much too small for so many," said Thomas. The children looked disappointed.

Suddenly I jumped up and shouted, "Everybody, listen to me." I had arrived at a bold decision.

The children looked at me expectantly.

"We'll use the electric stove in the kitchen in the inn," I announced.

"You always seem to forget that we have no electricity," scoffed Robert Pell.

"I've forgotten nothing," I said heatedly. "If we have no electricity, we will make some."

"How? Have you lost your mind? What do you mean?" There was a lot of yelling.

"Quiet," Thomas snapped. "Let the Professor finish. He was the one who knew how to print the posters."

"It's not so complicated," I said, scratching my nose thoughtfully. "The powerhouse is run with white coal."

"White coal! You're crazy," Gustav Tommel objected.

"Michael is nuts!" some of the girls snickered.

But the others wanted to know what I had in mind. "Shut up," they yelled to the rest.

"White coal is water power," I explained, adjusting my glasses. "Our powerhouse isn't run by a steam engine heated by coal, but instead by a turbine that is turned by the gravity flow of water. The turbine is coupled to a generator, and the generator makes electricity. Therefore, by making the turbine run, the generator is set into motion—so we can have electricity again."

"My goodness! How smart he is," squeaked Pussy Beck.

"All we have to do is find the right switches, and that shouldn't be too difficult," I said.

"Does that mean we would have light again tonight?" asked Thomas.

"Of course."

"Hurrah!" the children cried.

"I almost died of fright in the dark last night." Mimi Menken sighed.

"That's just too bad," said Thomas.

Mimi had been one of the worst during the tumult on Old Square.

Marianne looked at me challengingly. "May I ask how we're supposed to cook without water?" she inquired.

I grinned at her. "When we have electricity, we'll also have water. The pumps in the waterworks are run by electricity."

"How do we get into the powerhouse when we don't have the keys?" asked Thomas.

"Hm," I mumbled. "If we don't find the key, we'll have to break in."

"The keys to all the public utilities are in the Town Hall," volunteered Rick Randolph. "My father told me so." Rick's father was the janitor of the Town Hall.

"Boy, what a break!" I exclaimed.

The powerhouse is located on Circle Boulevard at the foot of Sunny Hill, and the waterworks are right next to it. I chose four boys, Emil Mansing, Irwin Bern, Gus Lamp, and Augie Donnek, to come with me. They're the smartest boys in my class, and I knew that I could rely on them. After I got the turbine going, these four were to stay and watch the instrument panels in both places. They were very flattered that I had picked them for such responsible jobs. On our way I impressed on them the importance of keeping their minds on their jobs and not allowing themselves to be distracted.

"We mustn't let anything go wrong," I said. "Your job is going to be very tiring, and I'll see that you're spelled after four hours."

"What do we do if something does go wrong?" Augie asked anxiously.

"Just turn everything off and phone me."

"Phone?" repeated Emil in astonishment. "There isn't any phone working. Mrs. Hessel and Mrs. Merk have gone with the other grownups." Mrs. Hessel and Mrs. Merk are the telephone operators at Timpetill's central switchboard.

"I can make it work again," I said. "There are only ninety-nine subscribers in town, and any halfway intelligent person should be able to handle that many connections."

"But where can we call you?" asked Gus Lamp.

"At the Town Hall."

Thomas and I had decided to establish headquarters for the "Fifteen Friends in Need" at the Town Hall. Everyone was to assemble in the Grand Hall, where we would read out our work program to them. That was the reason Thomas hadn't come with me. He had stayed behind in order to work out the most important work rules with the rest of the "Friends in Need." All the children below the age of eight had been sent to school. Olga Perl and Christine Herter, who were clever and sensible girls, were to watch over the young ones. They were going to read fairy tales to them or let them color pictures.

I had to hurry if I didn't want to miss the meeting in the Grand Hall, and I kept my fingers crossed that all would go smoothly in the powerhouse and at the waterworks. Emil Mansing and Gus Lamp were to stand watch in the power plant. Before we went inside, I pointed out the huge pipe made of corrugated iron that comes all the way down Sunny Hill and then disappears into the ground behind the powerhouse.

"The water comes shooting down inside this pipe until it hits the turbine with tremendous force," I told them. "The flow of water is regulated by a sliding valve."

"That means we'll have to open the valve first," said Emil.

I nodded and unlocked the entrance door.

The turbine room was light and clean. In the center stood the generator, linked to the turbine by means of a vertical drive shaft. On the left was the control desk, with all the controls and gauges.

First, I looked for the wheel that would turn the sliding valve. I found it not far from the generator. It looked like a steering wheel, mounted on an axle directly above the tile floor.

"That must be it," I said, and gave it a few turns to the right. It was hard to turn, and Emil and Irwin gave me a hand. We could hear a faint humming.

"The turbine is starting up," I cried.

"But where is the water?" asked Gus.

I had to laugh. "Deep down. That's where the turbine is located."

"Why don't you turn the wheel all the way?" asked Emil.

"Because we don't need much current for the time being," I answered. "The faster the turbine turns, the more electricity the generator makes. Tonight, when we'll need more electricity, we'll open the sliding valve further. You can tell how much electricity is being used by a gauge on the control desk. You have to see to it that the needle stays on the red mark in the center by regulating the valve."

We stepped up to the control panel, and I showed them the switches and gauges on the instrument panel.

"Where's the switch for the electric stove in the hotel?" asked Emil.

"It's all hooked up to the same system," I explained. "All the switches are marked."

I threw the main switch, and the lights in the turbine room went on.

"Look!" Gus exclaimed. "It works!"

"Marvelous!" Emil was spellbound.

"The pumps in the waterworks need a more powerful current," I explained, and threw another switch.

"Well, you're on your own now," I told them. "Don't let anybody in who doesn't know the password."

"What *is* the password?" both boys demanded.

"Up Timpetill." That was all I could think of on the spur of the moment.

I showed Irwin Bern and Augie Donnek what to do in the waterworks, then ran back to Old Square as fast as I could to reach the Town Hall in time for the meeting.

13

Two Presidents Make No Sense

Karl Benz beat the gong with a stick to signal the opening of the meeting. The gong was a cooky tin that Fritz Bollner had taken from his father's bakery. The hall was jammed with children, all laughing and talking at once, but when the gong sounded, they fell silent. We, the "Fifteen Friends in Need," were seated on the raised dais. In the middle sat Thomas, with Marianne on his left and me on his right.

Thomas rose. The children applauded as though he were a famous actor, and Karl once more sounded the gong.

When everyone had calmed down, Thomas began to speak. "Children of Timpetill." His voice sounded a bit unsteady, and he had to clear his throat a few times. Perhaps he had a little stage fright. "Children of Timpetill," he began again. "Our parents are still in hiding. Why they haven't come back by now is the big question."

Mimi Menken, who was sitting in the front row, jumped to her feet. "They're all dead," she wailed.

Karl pounded the gong, and, frightened, Mimi fell back into her seat.

"Our parents are *not* dead," Thomas replied. "They will certainly return."

He pretended to be sure of this, to reassure them. "But as long as they are gone," he continued, "we must see that peace and order are maintained in Timpetill. The Professor has started up the power plant and the waterworks so that we have light and water and can cook again."

"Three cheers for Michael!" cried the children.

"But there's lots more we have to do." Thomas seemed to have overcome his stage fright. He was talking fluently now. "We have to get right to work, or would you prefer to call on outsiders for help?"

"No!" shouted the children.

"You see, we knew how you'd feel. That's why we've made up an emergency work schedule. We want to keep the town going as best as we can until our parents return. In a little while we'll have a show of hands on whether you agree."

"Let's have it right now, Thomas," Fred Spitzer called.

"No, first we have to elect a president. Somebody has to direct things, or things will be helter-skelter."

The children jumped up. "Thomas and Michael should be presidents. Thomas and Michael!" they yelled, stamping with their feet.

"Wait! Listen to me!" I shouted.

Karl pounded his gong like mad, and at last the children calmed down.

"Two presidents make no sense," I said. "Thomas should be the only president. All in favor of Thomas raise their hands."

"Thomas, Thomas, Thomas!" they shouted in unison. All the children raised their hands.

"Thomas, that makes you president," I said.

"I accept the honor," Thomas said simply. "I hereby appoint you, Professor, as my chief executive."

The children cheered.

Thomas turned to the other "Friends in Need," who had been sitting on the dais.

"Please rise," he said.

The "Friends in Need" rose.

"Yesterday you were the first to help us establish order. I thereby appoint you all my captains."

The children applauded. It was a solemn moment. The newly appointed captains beamed. Fatso Paul was so carried away that he took a bow.

"Be seated," said Thomas, and the "Friends in Need" sat down. "Mark and Ernest, I appoint you as my personal aides."

"Gee, thanks," Mark stammered, visibly awed.

"Marianne," Thomas called.

"Here," reported Marianne.

"Marianne, you will be the captain in charge of food and hygiene."

"Great! But isn't there anything else I can do?"

"What does hygiene mean?" Irmgard Nisser had risen from her seat.

"Hygiene means bathing, brushing your teeth, cleaning your nails, combing your hair, doing your laundry, and so on," Marianne explained.

"Oh!" Irmgard sighed.

"Your office will be Room Number Two in the Town Hall," Thomas went on. "Paul Brandt is captain in charge of nutrition, and he'll be your assistant."

Fatso Paul rubbed his hands in glee. "We'll make sure that there is plenty of food. Marianne, how about it?" he called to her. The children howled with laughter. They all knew what a glutton Fatso Paul was.

Thomas signaled Karl Benz to sound his gong. Thomas was studying some notes, and when the children quieted down again, he said, "Kids, after the meeting is over, there'll be plenty for all of us to do. The streets have to be cleaned and the garbage has to be taken to the city dump in wheelbarrows. All the houses have to be tidied up and cleaned. The animals have to be fed, including the chickens, ducks, and geese. Mrs. Twilling's goat will have to be milked."

"We do that every evening," said Anna and Hannah, Mrs. Twilling's twin daughters.

"Good," said Thomas. Then he turned to Bob Pell, who sat on the dais. "Bob, did you feed the parrot?"

"I started to, but he bit my finger."

The children in the hall shrieked. Even Thomas grinned. "Why didn't you wear gloves?" he suggested.

He was about to continue reading from his emergency work schedule when Marianne stood up. "May I say something?" she asked.

"Marianne has the floor," I called.

"It's already eleven o'clock, Mr. President," she said. "If we're going to have lunch, we'd better start cooking, because it takes time to prepare food."

Thomas nodded in agreement.

"Who knows how to cook?" asked Marianne.

A dozen girls jumped up and eagerly waved their arms.

"I need a chief cook," said Marianne. "She can pick her own assistants."

"I'm a great cook!" cried Gerta Bartel.

"So am I," called Alice Putz.

"Alice, I appoint you chief cook," said Marianne.

"Why Alice?" demanded Gerta, pouting.

"Because Alice keeps her hands clean. Your fingernails are always dirty."

Gerta bit her lip and quickly sat down on her hands.

"Alice," Marianne continued, "pick your assistants and go over to the Red Kettle Inn right away. We're going to eat in three sections. Write down everything you use. I'll have the lists picked up later."

"What shall I cook?" Alice asked eagerly.

"Potato soup, hot dogs, and applesauce for dessert," Marianne ordered, without a moment's hesitation.

"What, potato soup again?" protested Fatso Paul.

"That's right," Marianne said firmly. "Potato soup

is easy to cook, and besides it's the only thing that will fill us up. The meats and vegetables aren't fresh anymore."

"My mother always gives me an apple for dessert," ventured Judith Lasko.

"You can do without it today, since you're getting applesauce."

Alice had chosen Monica Renzel, Berta Pirk, and plump Minna Hart as kitchen helpers. "Don't let anything burn," Fatso Paul called after them anxiously as they were leaving.

"We'll also need bread for breakfast," Marianne went on. "The doughnuts are all gone."

"Humph," grumbled Thomas. "Which girls know how to bake?"

Fritz Bollner jumped up. "I do," he said.

"Since when are you a girl?" inquired Thomas.

All the children broke out in laughter.

"But I do know how to bake," Fritz insisted, blushing.

"What can you bake?"

"Brownies," replied Fritz.

The children roared.

Thomas was angered. "Be quiet," he yelled, and Karl Benz pounded his cooky tin so hard that he almost dented it.

"It's not fair to make fun of Fritz," said Thomas.

"It's very decent of him to want to bake for all of us. Fritz, I appoint you honorary baking commissioner."

Fritz's face broke into a big grin.

"Can you bake bread?"

"Very well. As a matter of fact," said Fritz, "I often help my father when he bakes bread."

"How about blueberry muffins?" asked Marianne.

"I'm sorry. I don't know how."

"Too bad," said Marianne with a sigh.

"Kids—" Thomas was about to continue, but he stopped abruptly.

A big stone came flying through the open window and landed on the dais with a crash.

14

Lunch Is Now Being Served

Several boys climbed up on their chairs and looked out of the window. "There's Willy Stolz running across the square," exclaimed Arnold Picks.

"He's just disappearing into Church Street," reported Stefan Bottig.

"Let's run after him," cried some of the boys, eager to give battle.

"No," ordered Thomas. "Sit down. We have more important things to do."

Karl Benz picked up the stone and handed it to Thomas. The missile was wrapped in paper, which had something scrawled on it in red pencil. Thomas read it and laughed scornfully.

"Kids," he said, "Bloody Oscar thinks he's a big deal. He and the Pirates have sent us a message."

"Oh, read it, read it!" everybody called.

" 'To all the knuckleheads assembled in the Town

Hall,' " read Thomas. " 'The hour of revenge is approaching. Signed: The Chief of all Pirates, Oscar.' " Below the scribble was a crude drawing of a boy hanging from a gallows. An arrow pointed to the corpse; beside it was the name "Thomas."

Thomas tore up the paper and put the scraps in his pocket. "Kids, the Pirates are trying to scare us, but we won't let them. If they attack us, we'll know how to defend ourselves. Right?"

A storm of applause broke out.

"We'll give them the beating of their lives," shouted the boys. Even some of the girls joined in.

I was pleased. The picture had certainly changed. Only yesterday most of these same children would have fought against us, the "Friends in Need."

"We have to be prepared in case the Pirates try to ambush us," said Thomas. "We should have security guards. Volunteers, please step forward."

All of the boys jumped up as one man. "Me! Me! Me!"

Thomas raised his hand, and Karl struck the gong.

"We can use only the toughest and biggest," Thomas announced. "Officers of the Security Guard will be Max Wollinger, Otto Hoffman, and Karl Benz. It's up to them to select their men. The Professor and I are joint Commanders in Chief. All members of the guard will be armed with wooden sticks. They will patrol the streets and stand watch at Old Square. Two guards will be posted in the bell tower of the church at all times in order to keep a lookout for our parents. The moment they sight them, they will ring the bells so that we can assemble immediately in Old Square." Thomas picked up his notes again and studied them for a moment. "There will be a ten o'clock curfew. Everyone must be indoors by ten—children under eight by nine o'clock. The young ones will be cared for during the day by older girls."

Thomas turned to Rita Strauss and Karen Hoffman. "Rita and Karen," he said, "you are the captains in charge of Child Care. Olga Perl and Christine Herter will help you."

Karen ran over to Rita. They put their heads together and jabbered excitedly.

"We will all get up at six o'clock," Thomas went on firmly.

"What? At six?" shrieked Pussy Beck, horrified. "I'm still asleep then!"

"Anyone who isn't up will go without breakfast. Meals will be served in the Red Kettle Inn. Irma Kroeger and Albert Wollinger will be in charge of peace and order during mealtimes. Breakfast will be served for all at seven o'clock, but lunch and dinner will be served in several stages, so that every-one won't stop working at once. The workers will be organized into three groups—that goes for the boys in the Security Guard, too. The captains for the work detail are Kurt Kroeger and Bob Pell. Today, the first group will report for lunch at twelve, the second at one, and the third at two. For supper the second will be first, namely at five, the third will be second at six, and the first will be last at seven. Tomorrow the third group will eat lunch at twelve, the first at one, and the second at two. For supper the first will eat at five, the third at six, and the second at seven." Thomas took a deep breath. "Is that clear?"

"No!" the children shouted as if with one voice.

Thomas scratched his ear reflectively. "Hm," he muttered. "Ask your captains. They will explain it to you."

Kurt and Bob were completely at sea. They couldn't make any sense out of Thomas's meal schedule.

Thomas wanted to continue, but his voice had given out. "I've had it," he whispered hoarsely, shoving his notes over to me.

I rose, adjusted my glasses, and cleared my throat. "Boys and girls," I began. "We shall now vote on the emergency work detail."

But we never got that far. One of the hall doors flew open, and plump Minna Hart appeared in the doorway. "Lunch is now being served," she announced, giggling, and disappeared like lightning.

Immediately there was a wild stampede for the exit. Karl Benz sounded his gong, but nobody paid any attention. That was the end of the meeting in the Town Hall.

15

Everybody Has to Work

"Jumping Jehosophat!" I exclaimed. The dining room of the inn had turned into a madhouse. The children had gone berserk all over again. Everyone wanted to be first at the tables. They were fighting for seats as though their lives depended on it. Mimi Menken sat on the floor bawling—Anna and Hannah had pushed her off a bench. Fred Spitzer and Stefan Bottig were going at each other with their fists, while Hubert Sterzing had managed to clamber on the back of Arnold Picks, who had been lucky enough to gain a seat.

The little children were frightened and sat huddled in a corner. Olga Perl and Christine Herter had posted themselves in front of them protectively.

"Stop this fighting at once," I shouted. "Have you gone completely crazy?"

Startled, the children let go of one another.

"If you don't behave at once, you won't get anything to eat," croaked Thomas. He still didn't have his voice back.

"You ought to be ashamed," Marianne put in. "You're acting like cannibals."

"There isn't enough room at the tables," complained Fred Spitzer, panting.

"Is that a reason to act like maniacs? Besides, that was one of the reasons why you weren't all supposed to eat at once, but in three stages. Have you already forgotten that?"

"But the work groups haven't been organized yet," protested Gerhard Wilkins.

"I think the little ones should be fed first," Marianne proposed. "We should have a special seating for them."

Thomas nodded in agreement. "Everybody over eight go out on the square," he said hoarsely. "We'll call you when it's your turn. The captains will organize you into work groups while you wait."

Sullenly, the older children left, but no one dared to contradict. The captains for the work details and the Security Guard followed them.

"Rita and Karen," called Marianne. "Put the little ones at the table, and Olga and Christine will supervise them."

"Irma and Albert," said Thomas. "Stay at the

door and don't let anybody inside until the little ones have finished."

"I'll lock the door," said Irma.

"But when the older kids come in, how will we know who belongs to what group?" asked Albert.

"The captains will make a list of each group," I said. "You will get these lists, and everyone must call out his name when he enters. If someone's name is not on the list, he's not allowed to enter."

After that was settled, Thomas, Marianne, Mark, Paul, and I went into the kitchen to find out why the food wasn't being served yet. The kitchen staff was standing on their toes at the stove, stirring steaming pots with big wooden ladles. Alice had an apron tied around her waist, and a tall white chef's cap was perched askew on her head. She looked like a real kitchen chef. Her cheeks were flushed from the heat, and her left thumb was wrapped in a handkerchief. Apparently she had stuck it into the soup by mistake.

"Alice," said Marianne, "the little children will always be served first. Today they can have a pudding for dessert as a reward for being so good."

"Pudding?" Alice swept around indignantly, her hands on her hips. "I can't possibly cook a pudding now!"

"All right, all right," Marianne said hastily. "Then give each of them a piece of chocolate instead."

"Minna," commanded Alice, "get three big bars of chocolate from the storage room and put it on the list."

"We thought the food would be ready by now," said Thomas cautiously.

"It's been ready for half an hour," snapped Alice, mopping her forehead with her apron. "But we can't be expected to wait on table on top of everything else. We already have to peel potatoes, mince onions, open cans, dice carrots, wash dishes, cook, make out lists—what else do you want us to do? I need four waitresses."

"Paul," said Marianne, "go outside and get four strong girls and bring them here at once."

"Four strong girls, coming up!" Fatso Paul said cheerfully, and disappeared.

"Alice, may I taste the potato soup?" I asked. The soup smelled tantalizing.

"Scram! I have no use for you in the kitchen." We scrammed.

"It's better not to fool around with cooks," said Thomas somewhat meekly.

By now the young ones were seated at two long tables in the dining room, patiently waiting for food. Olga sat at the head of one of the tables and Christine at the other. Karen and Rita went busily from one child to the next, tying napkins around their necks. "Hi, Lotti, hi, Lisa!" Thomas had discovered Rita's little sisters and waved at them merrily.

"Hi," Lotti and Lisa piped in return, waving their soup spoons.

"You'll have something to eat soon. We're just waiting for the waitresses."

"Here they are," said Marianne. "Open the door, Irma. Here come the waitresses."

Fatso Paul and four sturdy girls squeezed through the door. They were Annette Vogler, Effi Deckel, Doris Hagenberg, and Judith Mollick, bursting with laughter because Fatso Paul was poking them with a stick, pretending he was herding a flock of geese.

"These are the strongest girls of Timpetill," he announced proudly. "Each of them is capable of lifting a bicycle with one hand."

"Please go into the kitchen and report to Alice," said Marianne to the girls.

Still giggling, the four waitresses disappeared.

"They didn't want to help at first," Paul told us, "but I told them that waitresses could have seconds. That did the trick."

"For heaven's sake," I burst out. "I almost forgot. I've got to get the telephone going. I'll need two telephone girls right away."

Out on Old Square, most of the children had been organized into work groups. The Security Guard was also almost complete. Its members, in military formation three rows deep, were lined up near the statue. They were armed with long sticks, which they had gathered in the gardens behind the houses.

I ran over to Kurt Kroeger, who was surrounded by the work crews. He had each child call out his name, and Bob Pell entered the names in a note-book.

"Excuse me," I said, interrupting him. "You have to let me have two girls for the telephone service."

"Take your pick," he said obligingly.

"How about Pussy Beck and Inge Laemmler?"

"Go ahead."

I knew that Pussy and Inge were very smart. Inge is the daughter of the president of the Timpetill Mortgage and Loan Association, and Pussy is the daughter of Mrs. Beck, the piano teacher. Inge is only eleven years old, but I chose her as a telephone operator because she has a nice, clear voice. Sometimes Pussy is a little fresh, but she is exceptionally intelligent.

"Both of you come with me, please," I called to them. They were happy to come along. This way they didn't have to clean streets or wash laundry.

"Is it difficult to be a telephone operator?" Inge asked eagerly.

"Don't worry," I said, "I'll explain it all."

The telephone office is on Main Street at the corner of Timpe Street, where the post office stands. We climbed up one flight of stairs and walked down a corridor. The telephone office is very small, and the switchboard is placed against the wall on the right. It looks like a desk with a tall box on top of it. The flat part of the desk contains two rows of plugs attached to cables. Between the operator and the row of plugs are small switches, one for each pair of plugs. The box rising above the desk has rows of holes in it, and each hole has a signal light and a telephone number above it.

I sat down and showed Pussy and Inge what to do.

"First, you put on the headset with the mouthpiece and the earphone and wait. When one of the lights flashes above one of the holes, you pull out one of the plugs in the back row and stick it into the hole with the light. Then you throw the switch in front of the plug and say, 'Number please.' After the caller has given you the number, you pull out the front plug and stick it into the hole with the right number on it. Now you have made the connection. Is that clear?"

"What fun!" Inge said, enraptured.

First Pussy and then Inge sat down at the switch-board and practiced until I was satisfied.

"Inge, you service the board first. Meanwhile, Pussy can go to eat and spell you in an hour."

"An hour?" Inge looked at me, horrified. "You mean that I will have to sit here all by myself for a whole hour?"

"Maybe I can get you a baby-sitter," I said mockingly.

"But nobody is using the telephone now."

"Never mind. You can never tell—Gus Lamp might call me from the powerhouse. Or Irwin from the waterworks. Somebody might call any minute, and the telephone is essential."

"But I'm afraid to be alone," whimpered Inge, looking ready to cry.

"How silly can you get?" I said. "The security guards are in constant readiness on Old Square. Nobody will hurt you. What's the matter with you, anyhow? This is an emergency, and we all have to work. You have to be here only for an hour. Mrs. Hessel and Mrs. Merk work eight hours every day, and Miss Klex, the night operator, sits here all night all by herself."

"But I'm not a regular operator," Inge said.

"You are now," I replied curtly. I felt sorry for

her, but I could not let her know it. It wasn't my fault that it didn't seem like such fun to her anymore. If everybody was going to do just what they liked, where would we be?

"Inge is very spoiled," Pussy said scornfully.

"I'm not," Inge protested, offended. She jumped up.

Fortunately, just then one of the signal lights flashed.

"Oh, dear," Inge exclaimed, and sat down quickly. "Somebody is making a call. What do I do?"

"Stick the rear plug into the hole where the light came on."

Inge did as I told her. "I still can't hear anything," she said.

"Throw the black switch forward," I hissed.

Inge pushed the switch. "What?" she called into the mouthpiece. "This is Inge. Who's Inge? Inge is me."

"I told you to say 'Number please,' " I whispered.

"I'm supposed to say 'Number please' " repeated Inge. "You don't need any number? It's Thomas," Inge said to me.

"Ask him what he wants," I said.

"Michael wants me to ask you what you want,"

said Inge. "Oh, dear! What's happened? Is it something awful?"

I snatched the headset from her and put it on.

"What's the matter, Thomas?"

"Come to the Town Hall quickly," Thomas barked "We're out of potatoes."

"Without potatoes we're lost," I grunted. "I'll be right over."

16

The Goose Bites and the Garbage Stinks

Children were scurrying busily about the Town Hall. The whole place looked like an anthill. They were dashing in and out of the different offices to get instructions from their captains.

Marianne was in Room Number Two. She sat behind a desk so huge that she was all but hidden from sight. She was talking to a group of boys and girls. Paul Brandt was seated opposite her. He was groaning and perspiring, trying to figure something out on a piece of paper while nibbling a cracker.

Thomas, as president, had established himself in Mayor Lomser's office. His aides, Mark and Ernest Werner, were with him.

"We're saved, Michael," he called as I stormed in. "Ernest tells me that there are lots of potatoes in a field outside the town. All we have to do is dig them."

"Thank goodness!" I exclaimed, relieved, and

slumped into a chair. I had torn across the square like a bolt of lightning. "How far is the field?"

"Just beyond the station," said Ernest Werner.

Marianne rushed in, waving a piece of paper in her hand. Fatso Paul was trailing behind her. "We shall need three hundred and fifty potatoes for the soup tonight," she called. "We've just figured it out."

"That means four to five sacks," Thomas said, wrinkling his forehead. "We can only fill the sacks half full or they'll be too heavy to carry."

"How are we going to get the sacks from the field to the inn?" I asked.

"In Mr. Wollinger's carriage," answered Thomas. "It's still in the alleyway of the dairy. All we have to do is get twenty or so boys from the Security Guard to push it, and we'll get the potatoes here in no time at all."

"Fine, let's get started," I said, getting up. "What are we waiting for?"

"We're waiting for our scouts," said Mark.

"Scouts? What scouts?"

"I sent Harold Treck and Norbert Knittel out on bicycles. They are security guards, and their mission is to find out where the Pirates are. We must make sure that we don't run into them while we're hauling potatoes."

"Can't we eat something while we're waiting for the scouts to return?" I asked, and sat down. I was exhausted and completely starved.

"We'll take some bread with us," said Marianne.

"Bread? Do we have bread?"

"Yes, Fritz Bollner has already baked twelve loaves."

"How did they turn out?"

"Awful," groaned Fatso Paul.

"They're not that bad," said Marianne. "He just forgot the salt."

Two girls burst excitedly through the door.

"Marianne, the geese are biting our legs," one of them cried indignantly.

"Why?" asked Marianne, perplexed.

"I don't know. They just don't like us."

"We belong to the Animal Feeding Brigade," explained the other girl. "We can't get near the feed sacks. Every time we try, the geese attack us. One goose bit Mimi and made her cry, but she's really being an awful baby about it. She's got nothing more than a little blue bruise."

Marianne pondered a moment, then brightened. "Go and get stilts from the toy shop. Then the geese won't be able to get at your legs."

"There are also three pigs in the pen," said one

of the girls. "They squeal and grunt because they are hungry. But we have no idea what to feed them."

"Oh, dear," said Marianne, rolling her eyes. "What *do* pigs eat?"

"Potato soup," said Fatso Paul sneeringly.

"I think they'll eat potato peels," I said.

"I bet that's exactly what they eat," said Thomas.

"Get the potato peels from the inn kitchen," Marianne told the girls.

No sooner had they disappeared than Fred Spitzer burst into the room. "The garbage stinks!" he cried.

"What garbage?" asked Marianne.

"All the garbage. I'm in charge of garbage collection. The children don't do what I tell them. They say they can't stand the smell."

"The garbage has to be removed," said Marianne. "Otherwise, we'll have millions of flies. Tell the children to hold their noses."

"That won't work," said Fred. "They need both hands to empty garbage cans."

"Tell them then to put clothespins on their noses. That will do it," I suggested.

"You've got it, Professor!" Fred Spitzer dashed out and on his way almost collided with two scouts.

"The Pirates are in the riding academy, Mr. President," reported Harold, giving a military salute.

"Cut out the formalities," said Thomas. "What are they doing there?"

"They're holding a council of war."

Thomas whistled through his teeth. "That means trouble! Were you able to listen?"

"No," reported Harold. "We sneaked up on them all right, but they had sentries posted. Two of them spotted us, and we had to retreat. They ran after us but couldn't catch us. We jumped on our bikes and pumped like fury."

"We'd better get this show on the road," said Thomas. "Let's go."

We dashed outside.

"I need twenty volunteers for a dangerous mission," Thomas called over to the Security Guard standing in the square. Almost half of them ran over. Thomas chose twenty boys. "You'd better come along, too," Thomas said to Max Wollinger. "We'll need the horse carriage."

We rushed over to the dairy, opened the gates to the court in the rear, and froze. The carriage was gone.

17

St. Matthew in a Car Accident

"For the love of Pete," Mark called, "where is the carriage?"

"Our carriage!" cried Max Wollinger. "When Father gets back and finds the carriage gone, he'll hit the roof."

"The Pirates must have stolen the carriage last night," I said. "That's as clear as crystal."

"Where could they have hidden it?" Marianne was crushed. She had been looking forward to riding on the coachman's box again.

"Should we make a search for it?" several of the security guards asked eagerly.

"No," said Thomas. "We have no time to spare. The Pirates are up to something. We'd better get back to Old Square as quickly as possible."

"If only we had a car," remarked Ernest Werner.

"No such luck," said Thomas. Our town has

only seven private cars, and their owners were wise enough to see that they were well locked up. "Besides, you're not supposed to take other people's cars and drive off with them," said Marianne.

"That's right," agreed Thomas, scratching himself behind the ear. "On the other hand, we can't let the children go without anything to eat. They've worked their heads off all day, and something has to be done about feeding them."

"There's always the herring in sour cream and the lobster tails that I saw in the inn refrigerator," Fatso Paul began.

"Stop this blabbering about herring and lobster tails," Thomas said, interrupting him. "Who wants to feed hungry children with herring in sour cream and lobster tails?"

"I know of an automobile that belongs to the town and that isn't locked up," I said.

"Which? What?" the others asked.

"The fire truck. It always stands ready at the fire house, and the doors are always open."

"Boy," said Thomas slowly. "That could be the solution."

"Hurrah! I'll drive it!" Fatso Paul called cheerily.

"That's what you think," Thomas growled at him.

"I wouldn't trust you with a baby carriage. Driving a car takes knowledge. Professor, do you happen to know how to drive?" He looked at me hopefully.

"Naturally," I said brazenly. I knew a lot about cars from books, but I had never driven anything except for the few times my Uncle Adolf had let me drive his tractor.

"These fire trucks are like wild horses, you know."

"Don't worry," I said. "I'll drive slowly and I'll watch out."

The fire department is on Main Street, four blocks from Old Square. We made it there in five minutes and stood admiringly in front of the fire engine. It looked beautiful and impressive, its bright red paint gleaming from loving care. To be allowed to ride in this truck someday was every child's dream. At last our chance had come.

I climbed into the driver's seat, and Marianne sat down beside me with complete trust.

"The steering wheel is as big as a wagon wheel," she remarked.

"Maybe we'd better first push the monster out of the garage," Thomas called up to me.

I nodded. I confess that my heart had begun to pound. The sight of the long levers at my side and all the buttons and gauges on the dashboard suddenly made me nervous.

The boys leaned all their weight against the back of the truck. It did not budge.

"Professor, why won't it move?" Thomas called between gasps.

"I don't know. Try again."

The boys coughed, groaned, and complained loudly, but nothing happened.

"Did you release the handbrake?" called Thomas.

"No," I admitted. "I forgot."

"Knucklehead! I thought you knew how to drive."

"That can happen to any driver," I retorted hotly.

I pushed forward the big lever at my left, and the fire truck slowly rolled out on the street. I pulled the handbrake to stop it.

The boys surrounded the truck and stared at me.

"Now what?" said Thomas.

"First, I have to start the motor."

"OK. Go ahead."

"Take it easy. I haven't found the starter button yet." I pulled several knobs on the dashboard. The windshield wipers began to flap, the headlights flashed on, the directional signals started to flicker, and the siren let out an earsplitting wail. Only the motor remained dead.

"It won't start," I said, perplexed.

"Maybe it's out of gas," suggested Ernest Werner.

"Fire trucks are always full of gas," I replied, irritated. "Besides, that has nothing to do with the starter." I pushed the knobs in. The windshield wipers stopped, the lights went out, the turn signals ceased to flicker, and the sirens died down. But the motor remained dead.

"Funny," I said, "something must be wrong." My eyes fell on a keyhole in the dashboard. "What a dope I am," I cried. "Quick, look for the ignition key. It should be hanging on a board somewhere in the station."

Several members of the Security Guard ran inside the station house. Meanwhile, I took a closer look at everything.

"What are those two big pedals for on the floor?" asked Mark.

"Those are the brakes," Fatso Paul explained importantly. "The left pedal works the brakes on the left wheels, and the right works the right wheels."

"You don't know much about cars, stupid. The left pedal is the clutch, the right one the brake," I said.

"What's the small pedal for?" asked Marianne.

"That's to give it gas."

"It looks complicated," Marianne said and sighed. But she stayed bravely in her seat.

"We've found a key," said Gerhard Humbold, and handed one to me. I stuck it in the keyhole. It was the right one!

"It fits," I said. I turned it, pressed the button next to it, and the motor started up with a deep roar.

"Hurrah!" shouted the boys.

"Drive to Old Square first, Michael," Thomas ordered. "We have to get the sacks and the loaves of bread."

The boys wanted to jump on the running boards, but Thomas would not allow it. "The Professor should try it alone, first—just to be on the safe side. Marianne, you'd better get off, too."

"I'm not afraid," Marianne said stoutly.

I pushed down the clutch, put the car into gear, pressed the accelerator, and then let in the clutch. The truck lurched forward. I would have landed in the window of Mr. Meyer's toy shop if I had not frantically slammed on the brakes at the last moment. We stopped so abruptly that Marianne was thrown forward.

"Ouch," she cried, and clutched her forehead. She had banged her head against the dashboard.

"Are you hurt?" I asked, alarmed.

"I think I'll have a bump," she said, and looked at me reproachfully. "Do you have to drive so roughly?"

"I let the clutch in too fast. It ought to be done gently."

Suddenly Thomas was beside me. "Wouldn't it be a good idea if we forgot about the potatoes?" he asked.

"Chicken?" I said.

I put the truck into first gear again and drove off. Slowly I made my way down Main Street. For some reason, I couldn't steer straight. The truck lurched from side to side as if it had had too much to drink.

"Why do you zigzag so much?" Marianne asked, her eyes wide.

"I want to try out the steering," I lied, fighting the wheel.

The boys ran along at a respectful distance.

"Straight! Steer straight!" Thomas yelled, beside himself.

"I will," I called back. But not until we had reached the square was I able to hold a fairly steady course. I pushed the button for the siren and made for the inn. The excitement on the square had reached fever pitch.

"The fire truck! The fire truck!" Children came running from all directions. "Michael is driving the fire truck!"

"Keep back! Keep back!" Thomas yelled at the top of his voice. He had caught up with me and leaped on the running board. I circled and stopped in front of the inn. The children surrounded us. "Let us come, too," they begged.

"No, no," protested Thomas. "This isn't a joy-ride. We have to get potatoes."

Even the twenty boys whom we had picked to push the carriage had to stay behind.

"You have to help stand guard at the square," said Thomas. "That's more important."

The boys were disappointed. Only Max, Ernest, Fatso Paul, Mark, Marianne, Thomas, and I went on the potato hunt. But first we stopped to pick up bread and the empty sacks. Once more I took my seat at the wheel, and Marianne and Thomas sat beside me. The others jumped on the running boards and held on to the bars.

"Let's go, Professor," Thomas ordered.

I put the truck into gear but unfortunately shifted into reverse, so that we began to back up in the direction of the statue.

"Stop, stop!" everybody shouted.

I wanted to step on the brakes but hit the gas pedal instead, and the truck bashed like a battering ram against the statue of St. Matthew.

Cries of horror rang across the square. St. Matthew tottered dangerously for a moment, then settled back into place.

"Wow!" gasped Thomas. "You almost knocked down St. Matthew."

We jumped from the truck and stared. St. Matthew was miraculously unharmed. Only the tip of his toe was broken off.

18

In a Bad Pinch

"Digging potatoes is a killer," groaned Fatso Paul, slapping furiously at a horsefly that wanted to land on his cheek.

Flies were swarming all around us. The heat in the potato field was stifling. The soil was still moist from the rain the night before, and our hands and shoes were caked with mud. Marianne sat on the empty sacks, counting the potatoes as we threw them on a pile. She had borrowed my handkerchief and tied it around her head to keep her hair from falling in her face. It made her look like a peasant girl.

"Three hundred and ten, three hundred and eleven, three hundred and twelve . . ." she counted aloud. "Help, what's that?" she suddenly cried out.

Thomas glanced up casually. He had just pulled a potato from the ground and was carefully scraping mud off it.

"A frog," he said. "Haven't you ever seen a frog before?"

"I've seen millions," she said, piqued. "But this one is covered with warts."

"That's because it's a toad," explained Thomas.

"Please go away, toad," Marianne told the toad. She obviously didn't dare touch it.

I tossed a tiny potato at the toad, and it took one leap and disappeared. Marianne gave a sigh of relief, but then she appeared to be lost in sad thoughts.

"If only I knew where Daddy and Mummy are," she said suddenly.

We were at a loss as to what to say.

"We just can't go on living without our parents," she continued.

"If they aren't here by tomorrow, we shall go and look for them," promised Thomas, with a catch in his voice.

"Do you really mean it?"

"I promise, Marianne."

Doggedly, we concentrated on digging potatoes.

"Oh, oh, oh!" howled Max Wollinger, and jumped up and down on one leg, whimpering.

"What's the matter?" we asked.

"I almost cut off my toe with the spade."

We had found the spades on the fire truck. Mark Himmel, who had turned to look at Max, suddenly cried out, "Jeepers, I can't stand straight!" He looked at us helplessly, bent over his spade.

"Why not?" asked Marianne, full of concern.

"I don't know. I think I've broken my back."

"Nonsense," said Thomas. "You have a stiff back from bending over. My back hurts, too."

"Isn't there anything we could eat tonight besides potato soup?" complained Fatso Paul. Perspiration dripped from his nose.

"You can quit now," Marianne announced triumphantly. "We've got enough potatoes. In fact, we have three hundred and fifty-two."

"Hurrah!" Ernest Werner cried, full of exuberance, and flung a potato into the air. It came down on Thomas's head. We all laughed. Only Thomas didn't think it was so funny.

When we calmed down, we filled the sacks with potatoes and dragged them up the embankment, then lifted them across the tracks and dragged them again to the station plaza, where the fire truck was parked alongside the tracks. As we turned the corner at the station, we spotted a number of boys running off. They disappeared into the bushes not far from the riding academy.

"Nuts," said Thomas. "Those were Pirate spies. Too bad they discovered us. Now we've got to beat it."

We loaded the sacks hurriedly on the truck. I seated myself at the wheel, and Marianne and Thomas took their places beside me.

The others jumped on the running board.

"Hold on. Here we go!" I called.

"Stop!" Max yelled. "Don't start, Michael."

"Why not?"

"The left front tire is flat."

We leaped off and stared at the flat tire.

"The Pirates did that," I said. "The valve cap is missing. They took it to let the air out."

"Will we have to walk now?" Fatso Paul asked, blanching.

"The potatoes—" Marianne looked at the sacks with consternation. "We can't let the potatoes go."

"I'm afraid we're in a tough spot," said Thomas gloomily.

We stood between the streetcar tracks, not knowing what to do. Then I had an idea. "Hold everything," I shouted.

"What's up?" the others demanded, full of curiosity.

Smugly I rubbed my hands. "Let's try and pull a fast one on the Pirates. If we can't use the fire truck, we'll go back to Old Square on the trolley. It's over there in the shed. After all, what's a trolley for?"

Marianne jumped up and down with excitement. "Oh, how wonderful! We can save the potatoes."

"And we won't have to walk," Fatso Paul pointed out with a grin.

"Ernest," I said, "run over to the station and call the powerhouse. Tell them to turn on the high tension current for the streetcar system."

The rest of us ran over to the streetcar shed and joined forces to slide open the back door. Behind it stood the venerable trolley, which for many years now had shuttled back and forth between the station and Old Square. We all hoped that it would never cease to operate because we were very fond of it.

I went all the way to the rear to let up the contact slider until it connected with the overhead wire. Then I mounted the front platform to man the controls. This time I was determined not to make any mistakes. As a matter of fact, I knew a lot more about trolleys than fire trucks. Every time I rode on our streetcar, Mr. Fink, the motorman, explained the meaning of the different levers.

I climbed into the motorman's cab. There is a console with a control lever that regulates the speed. It also regulates the counter current, used in braking. Then there is another large lever, which is the handbrake.

The others stood behind me and watched, full of curiosity.

"Why doesn't it start?" asked Marianne.

"I'm waiting for the current. We can't move without electricity. When the electricity is connected, the lamp above us lights up."

Our eyes were fixed impatiently on the lamp, but it remained dark.

"Why the devil does it take so long?" I asked tensely.

Just then Ernest appeared at the door of the shed. "Michael," he reported in a quivering voice, "I can't reach the powerhouse."

"Why not? What's up?" I said apprehensively.

"The operator doesn't answer."

19

The Telephone Operator Doesn't Answer

"What?" I cried, shocked. "The operator doesn't answer? That's the limit. Just when we need the telephone so urgently!" I jumped off the streetcar and darted over to the station. In the stationmaster's office I grabbed the receiver and listened tensely. It was true, the line was dead. I jiggled the receiver furiously and hung on.

At last Pussy Beck answered. "This is the operator," she said. "What do you want?"

"This is Michael. Why didn't you answer at once?" I demanded.

"I did," she protested.

"That's a lie."

"It is not. You're lying."

"No, you're the one who's lying. We've been trying to reach you for the past fifteen minutes."

"That's not my fault. That must have been Inge. I've just come on. She was asleep when I arrived."

"That's the limit. Here we are in terrible danger, with the Pirates about to pounce on us, and Inge sleeps on her job. Connect me with the powerhouse at once."

"But I don't know the number," Pussy said, annoyed.

"Oh, that's right. Wait . . ." I looked it up in the telephone directory, which fortunately was lying nearby. I found the number in no time. The telephone directory of Timpetill consists of two pages, one of which is given over to advertisements. "The number of the powerhouse is eighty-five," I said.

"Eighty-five, eighty-five," repeated Pussy. "Eighty-five, let's see . . ."

"Well, are you going to connect me one of these days? Hurry up."

"Take it easy. Eighty-five . . . first I have to find the right plug."

"Hello?" A boy's voice came over the phone.

I breathed again. "This is Michael. Let me have the high tension juice at once," I barked excitedly.

"I don't have any high tension juice," the voice replied.

"Are you crazy? Of course you have high tension power. It's the big lever on your right."

"There is no big lever on my right. We never

had high-voltage electricity. The oven gets red hot without it."

"What oven?" I asked, dumfounded. "Who is this?"

"This is Fritz Bollner at the bakery."

"Oh, rats! Please hang up. I've got the wrong number."

"What number did you want?"

"Eighty-five."

"Ha, ha." Fritz laughed. "This is fifty-eight."

"Oh, dear," Pussy cut in. "I got the numbers turned around."

"Why aren't you more careful? Some operator you are!"

"You don't have to be so rude," protested Pussy.

"You nitwit, you can't even keep two numbers straight in that brain of yours."

"One more word out of you and I won't connect you at all," screamed Pussy.

"You dare and I'll have you arrested on the spot," I yelled.

"Ha, ha," Pussy sneered. "The Professor has gone bats."

"Shut up!" I cried, hardly able to contain myself.

"Why?" asked a boy's voice.

"Who's this?" I croaked.

"Gus. This is the powerhouse."

"Thank heaven! Please turn on the high voltage for the streetcar right away."

"OK. That's the big lever on my right. Say, when are we going to be relieved?"

"Soon. I'll call you again later."

"What for?"

"Just to see if the telephone service is working."

"It seems to be working beautifully," Gus said, and hung up.

"Idiot," I mumbled as I raced back to the shed.

"Michael, the lamp is on," Marianne called to me. "Now we can start." She was looking forward to the trolley ride.

I jumped onto the platform, stood before the controls with my feet apart, and turned on the starter switch. Then I disengaged and turned the control lever to position number one. With that, the car moved out of the shed slowly.

"Hey, we're on our way!" Marianne called, her eyes fixed with wonderment on the tracks, which slid away beneath us.

I stepped on the floor bell, a metal knob on the floor, and the bell sounded ding, ding. There was not a soul in sight, but foresight is better than hindsight, I thought.

"Just take it nice and easy, Professor," Thomas called. He had become a bit leary of my driving since my first attempt with the fire truck.

"Everything is under control, chum," I said, and picked up a little speed.

"May I ring the bell?" asked Marianne.

"Sure," I said magnanimously, "but not now. Only when you can see someone in the street."

Fatso Paul, Mark, Ernest, and Max had more confidence in me than Thomas. Grateful for a chance to rest at last after their strenuous work, they were lounging on the car benches as if it were a Pullman. But the state of bliss was of short duration. I turned the control to "Off," applied the counter current, pulled on the handbrake, and we came to a smooth stop alongside the fire truck.

"We have to transfer the potato sacks," I called, jumping off the car.

"On the double, you lazybones," Thomas yelled. "Everybody give a hand."

We dragged the sacks over to the trolley and stowed them inside, then started up again. When we reached the boulevard, I turned the control to the number three position, and the trolley rattled along at a good speed.

"Oh, this is great!" Marianne exclaimed. Her cheeks were flushed, and her hair was flying around her face. Suddenly she stamped on the bell with such vigor that I braked like mad. Fatso Paul tumbled from the bench and landed hard on the floor.

"You weren't to ring the bell, Marianne," I scolded her.

"But there's someone ahead of us," she protested. Far away we could now see a boy on a bicycle racing toward us. As he came nearer, we recognized Norbert Knittel, one of our Security Guard scouts.

I applied the brake again and came to a complete stop. In no time, Norbert reached us. "Thomas, Thomas, quick," he shouted.

"What's happened?" asked Thomas.

"The Pirates are marching through Mill Street onto Old Square," panted Norbert.

20

Potatoes Zoom through the Air

"Let her wide open, Michael," Thomas ordered. "We have to get ahead of the Pirates."

I turned the control all the way to the left, to position five, and we hurtled down Main Street like a streamliner. Trees and houses flashed past us. "Ding, ding, ding." Marianne kept stepping on the bell to warn all children who were busy sweeping the sidewalks or carting off the garbage. They stared at us, their mouths wide open.

Thomas leaned out of the window with his hair blowing in the wind. "Hide in your houses and lock the doors! The Pirates are coming!"

Like lightning, the children disappeared, slamming the doors shut after them.

Three blocks from Old Square, I reduced speed. At this point, Main Street goes uphill, until it reaches the square. I turned the control to "Off" and applied the counter current, stopping the car just before the end of the line. I pulled on the handbrake and turned off the electricity, and just to play it safe, I removed the control handle and put it in my pocket.

No sooner had we stepped off the car than we were surrounded by an excited group of our security guards.

"The Pirates are hiding in Church Street. They are armed with sticks," reported Otto Hoffman.

"We ordered all the girls to lock themselves in the inn," said Karl Benz.

Thomas praised him. "That was good thinking. We can't have girls around if there's going to be a fight." He turned to Marianne. "Marianne, you must go to the inn right away, too."

Marianne threw up her chin. Her eyes sparkled. "No," she said. "First, we must get the potatoes into the inn. Alice has to start cooking."

"Don't be pigheaded, Marianne," he snapped. "The potatoes can wait. The Pirates will be here any moment now. Run! Quick!"

It was too late. Just at this moment, the Pirates came pouring into the square from Church Street and ran toward us, shouting and swinging their sticks. Bloody Oscar and his aides, Willy Stolz and Hans Lomser, were in the lead.

"Let's go. Follow me!" Thomas called to us, and ran toward them. We fell in behind him and clashed with the Pirates in the center of the square. Sticks crashed down, fists flailed, and howls of pain arose from every side. Thomas and Oscar were locked in a stranglehold. I hurled myself on Willy Stolz. I had had it in for him for some time. It was he who had gotten us into all this trouble in the first place by tying the clock to the tail of Peter the cat. I held him in a bear hug and then threw him to the ground. "Give up?" I snarled.

"Yes, yes, I give up," he whined, and began to blubber.

I loosened my grip, intending to lead him off as my prisoner and lock him up somewhere in the Town Hall, but the little sneak kicked me in the shins and ran away. I was about to go after him in hot pursuit, but someone socked me on the nose and my eyeglasses flew to the ground. I stooped to pick them up. Luckily, they weren't broken, or I would have been in a fix, because I am very nearsighted. I was just about to straighten up when a boy came down on me like a ton of bricks, and I collapsed under him.

"Give up?" a voice grunted fiercely. It was Fatso Paul.

"Are you crazy?" I groaned, nearly suffocated. "It's me, Michael."

"Phooey," he grumbled, and rolled off of me. "I didn't recognize you from behind."

He gave me an embarrassed grin and then threw himself anew into the fracas, bowling over the nearest unlucky Pirate like a steamroller. I straightened my glasses and looked around. The battle was seesawing. The Pirates fought like madmen, but we wouldn't yield an inch. To my horror, I spotted Marianne in the thick of the melee. I had forgotten all about her in the heat of the battle. Willy Stolz and Hans Lomser were clutching her by the arms, and she was fighting them like a wildcat. "Let go of me, you cowards!" she shrieked.

"I'm coming, Marianne," I shouted, and tried to push my way through the throng. But a couple of Pirates flung themselves on me, and I had to fight desperately to defend myself. "Thomas!" I yelled. "Help Marianne!" But Thomas was rolling on the ground with Bloody Oscar.

"Let me go, you idiots!" I heard Marianne snarl. Willy and Hans were dragging her off as a prisoner. Marianne was in a bad spot.

At that moment, the door to the inn flew open, and out shot Alice and the four hefty waitresses. Alice was swinging an empty cooking pot, and the others were armed with long kitchen spoons and wet dish towels. Swinging their weapons right and left, they forced their way like ramrods through to where Marianne was struggling. Alice jammed the pot over Willy's head, and Hans got a working over with the spoons and the wet dish towels. Both boys took flight. The girls surrounded Marianne like bodyguards and began to lead her toward the inn, but she would have none of it. "I've got to take care of them myself," she cried. But Alice and her hefty crew grabbed their captain and dragged her, still protesting, to safety in the inn.

When the Pirates saw that Willy and Hans were taking off, they, too, took to their heels, leaving their chief behind. Oscar tore himself away from Thomas and dashed after them, foaming with rage.

"Come back here!" he howled in vain at his disappearing lieutenants.

Shouting and cheering, we ran after them. But we cheered too soon. The Pirates retreated as far as Main Street, where they discovered the trolley and our potatoes. We were greeted with a veritable hailstorm of potatoes and fled back to Old Square. The missiles were so painful that we could not even pick them up and throw them back at the enemy. Meantime, the Pirates were stuffing their pockets full of potatoes and continuing their attack.

"Surrender!" Oscar jeered.

We crouched behind the statue, behind lamp-posts and trees, and many potatoes landed harmlessly on the pavement. A few went crashing through windowpanes.

"Things look bad," I whispered to Thomas, gasping for breath. He and Fatso Paul were kneeling behind me by the statue.

"We've got to hang on," Thomas hissed back defiantly.

"Their ammunition can't last forever."

"Unfortunately, there are enough potatoes in the trolley to give us a very hard time," I said. "If they get the bright idea of attacking our flank, we're lost."

"Look!" called Karl. He was pointing to a house standing at the corner not far from the streetcar. Mark Himmel was peeking out of a window on the second floor. He must have sneaked through the back yards without being seen by the Pirates. Now he climbed to the windowsill and braced himself to jump. About six feet below him was the roof of the trolley.

"What is he up to?" groaned Fatso Paul. "He must have gone mad."

Just then Mark took a bold leap and landed on the roof of the car. He let himself nimbly down onto the platform. Frantically, he tugged at the big hand-brake. The trolley began to roll backwards downhill, slowly at first, then gathering speed. Seeing their valuable ammunition slide away, the Pirates let out a howl of fury. They gave chase, but before they were able to catch up with the trolley, it had rolled far away to the corner of Crooked Road, where it finally came to a standstill.

"We must rescue Mark," Thomas called to us, and dashed off toward the Pirates. The rest of us swiftly snatched up what potatoes were nearest and then followed him as fast as our legs would take us. Unfortunately, the Pirate chief, followed by his aides, reached the trolley before we did. He jumped onto the platform to grab Mark, but Mark had the presence of mind to throw a potato squarely into his

face. Oscar reeled backward, pulling Willy and Hans with him. Before they managed to disentangle themselves, we attacked the other Pirates from the rear, bombarding them mercilessly with potatoes. They soon panicked and made off through the side streets.

Oscar, Willy, and Hans were still sitting on the pavement, glaring at us dazedly.

"You'd better surrender, Oscar!" said Thomas threateningly. "You're licked."

"You were lucky," Bloody Oscar retorted sulkily, tenderly feeling his nose. It was red and swollen—evidently Mark had scored a bull's-eye.

"If Mark hadn't stolen the trolley, you would have been the ones who got licked."

"Cut out the excuses, wise guy," I puffed, completely out of breath. Never in my life had I run as fast as when we chased the Pirates to save Mark.

"Karl," ordered Thomas, "take a detachment of the Security Guard and lead these three Pirate bums to the Town Hall. Lock them up in the cellar and post four men as sentries."

"Right," panted Karl. "I'll see to it that they won't get away."

Karl Benz and twelve security guards led Oscar, Willy, and Hans away, and at last we had time to look after Mark. He sat motionless on the steps of the trolley.

"Mark," said Thomas, "what you did with the trolley was stupendous."

"Well, I wanted to help somehow," said Mark. "You didn't want me to be part of the fighting team."

"You saved the day for us, Mark," I said.

Mark remained silent and cautiously climbed down to the pavement. He bit his lips and stood on one leg.

"Why are you standing on one leg?" I asked.

"My left foot hurts like the devil," he murmured.

Thomas and I grasped him under the arms, and he hobbled between us over to Old Square.

All the girls, their faces aglow, were running toward us.

"Hail to the victors!" Marianne cried ecstatically. "Now we have to hurry and pick up all the potatoes."

We let go of Mark, who collapsed to the ground.

"Mark, what's the matter?" Marianne was shaken.

"He says that something is wrong with his left foot," I said, nervously adjusting my glasses.

Marianne kneeled down beside Mark and took off his shoe and sock. "Oh, dear, that does look bad!" she exclaimed. "Your ankle is all brown and green."

Mark sat up. "Is it fatal?" he breathed.

"Not a chance," said Thomas. "You just sprained

your ankle when you jumped on the roof of the streetcar."

"I wish my parents were here," moaned Mark.

All the children fell silent. We were all thinking the same thing. Where were our parents? Why didn't they come back?

Marianne cleared her throat. "Don't be sad, Mark," she said. "You're a hero now. And as a reward, you will get a whole bar of chocolate all to yourself."

"Thanks," Mark said, deeply moved.

21

The Trial

"Bring in the accused," Thomas intoned solemnly.

We were gathered at the Arena in order to try the Pirate chief and his two aides. Karl Benz sounded the cooky tin that he had brought along. Everybody's eyes were glued expectantly on the door to the stables, behind which Oscar, Willy, and Hans were waiting to be brought in.

Thomas, Marianne, and I sat on crates in the center of the Arena. Beside Thomas we had planted a pole that served as a flagstaff for the president's standard—a piece of cardboard on which we had painted Timpetill's coat of arms. The captains formed a semicircle behind us, all standing except Mark Himmel. Around Mark's ankle Marianne had wrapped a thick bandage, of which he was very proud. About three paces in front of us a wooden board lay across piles of brick. It served as the defendants' bench.

We had purposely chosen the Arena for the trial

because it had been the Pirates' headquarters. We wanted to demonstrate to all the children of Timpetill that the reign of the Pirates had come to an end.

The Arena was jammed. All the children had come in order to be present at the moment of retribution. The Pirates were scattered among them, looking very meek. After their unconditional surrender, they were very shamefaced. On their solemn promise that they would behave in the future, we had pardoned them, but we could not let Oscar, Willy, and Hans get off scot-free. After all, they were the chief culprits and had gotten us into all this trouble. One cannot always be lenient. Thomas had insisted that first Old Square be cleaned up after the big battle, so by the time we assembled in the Arena, the sun was already setting. The former Pirates had been pressed into service for the clean-up. They were made to gather all the potatoes and carry them into the inn. They had to sweep up the broken window glass and cart it off to the town dump. Finally we sent them to the station plaza to pump up the fire truck's flat tire.

Meanwhile, we still had to fix up the statue of St. Matthew. We found the piece of his toe that had broken off and glued it back where it belonged.

Since then, his toe has looked a bit crooked, but fortunately nobody seems to notice.

I drove the trolley back to its shed and the fire truck to the fire house. At the last minute, we remembered the carriage. We discovered that Oscar, Willy, and Hans had hidden it in the cemetery during the night. Max and Albert Wollinger got the horse, and the carriage was driven home. To Marianne's great joy, the horse had recovered from its cough.

All that time, Oscar, Willy, and Hans had been sitting under lock and key until we moved them to the Arena, where we locked them in the stables. Now we waited for their entry.

Someone leaped up and shouted, "Here they come!" Six of the strongest and tallest security guards were leading the Pirate chief and his lieutenants into the Arena.

"Boo, boo, boo!" It sounded from all sides, and Oscar, Willy, and Hans ducked instinctively. They were told to sit down on the defendants' bench, and their guards posted themselves immediately behind them.

Karl sounded the gong again, and I rose. I had been appointed public prosecutor and therefore had to speak first. Thomas and Marianne were the judges, and we also had an attorney for the defense. Every criminal, no matter how wicked, can ask for an attorney to defend him, Thomas had insisted. Lotte Dronte had voluntarily assumed the case for the defendants. She is the daughter of a local judge and thinks she knows something about legal procedure.

I straightened my glasses and cleared my throat. "Oscar," I began, "you have led astray the children of Timpetill and encouraged them to plunder shops. You incited them to steal apples, pears, and eggs. You also went rowing in the boats without permission."

"But there was no boat attendant," interrupted Oscar.

"Silence!" thundered Thomas.

"Oscar," I continued, "you hid the carriage in the cemetery to make things tough for us, and you let the air out of the tire of the fire truck to prevent us from using it."

"I had nothing to do with the tire," Oscar protested. "Blame Fritz Arnfeld and Peter Grump for that."

"Silence!" repeated Thomas. "You are only to speak when you are asked a question."

"Oscar," I said in a solemn voice, "you have always been a troublemaker in Timpetill, and you have carried it so far that our parents have abandoned us and made orphans of us. We have no idea where they are or whether we'll ever see them again."

Everybody jumped up. "Give him what's coming to him!" they called. "We want our parents back!" The former Pirates were yelling the loudest.

"Be quiet!" ordered Thomas. "You mustn't interfere with the trial. Sit down!"

Karl Benz pounded his gong, and the children sat down again.

"Oscar," I said, "you were a dirty rat to attack us on Old Square and bombard us with potatoes that were meant to go into our soup. You are also the cause of Mark Himmel's sprained ankle, so that now he has to limp on one foot. What have you to say in your defense?"

"You're just trying to make yourself important," Oscar blustered.

"Oscar is innocent," Lotte Dronte put in quickly.

"Fiddle dee dee," growled Thomas, and Lotte fell into an embarrassed silence.

"Willy Stolz," I said, "you tied an alarm clock on Peter the cat's tail. What have you to say in your defense?"

"But you watched me from the window without saying anything," said Willy.

"Don't get fresh," I said angrily. "If I had been on the square, I would have stopped you all right."

Lotte came to Willy's aid. "Willy is very fond of animals. I know that for a fact. I've seen him myself, scratching Peter behind his ears."

"You're just making that up," I said to her. "Nobody who loves animals would tie an alarm clock to a cat's tail. Hans Lomser!" I called. Hans started nervously; perhaps he had been dozing. "Hans," I said, "you and Willy tried to get rough with Marianne."

"She was resisting arrest," said Hans.

"You never would have succeeded!" Marianne cried.

"Hans," I said, "you were a party to all Oscar's misdeeds. What have you got to say in your own defense?"

"What do you mean?" stammered Hans.

"His father is our mayor," said Lotte.

"What has that got to do with it?" I demanded.

"That makes it even worse," said Thomas. "Being the son of the mayor does not give Hans any special dispensation."

"He's stupid," Lotte said in his defense.

"I am not stupid!" Hans hissed. "You're stupid yourself."

"Hold your tongue!" said Thomas. "I shall now pronounce the verdict. Have you anything else to say?"

"I plead mitigating circumstances for the defendant," said Lotte.

"Why?" asked Thomas.

"Because," said Lotte. "After all, I am his defense attorney."

"Overruled," said Thomas. To tell the truth, we had already decided on the punishments for Oscar, Willy, and Hans before the trial began. "The accused will rise," said Thomas sternly.

The three Pirates hesitated, but their guards gave them a rough prod, and quickly they stood up.

"Willy and Hans are sentenced to peel potatoes in the Red Kettle Inn," announced Thomas.

The children all around were crestfallen.

"Is that all?" squeaked Minnie Cobb. "I have to peel potatoes all the time at home!"

"But they will have to peel three hundred and fifty-two potatoes," Marianne pointed out.

"Unfortunately the number of potatoes has dwindled to three hundred and forty-seven," I interjected. We had been unable to locate five.

"Silence!" said Thomas. "Oscar, you are to be expelled from the community of the children of Timpetill. Nobody shall be allowed to talk to you, nobody shall play with you. You shall receive your meals in the backyard of the inn."

Oscar looked aghast. Then he covered his face

with his hands and burst into tears. The children were thunderstruck. Bloody Oscar, the great Pirate chief, crying! The sentence had hit him harder than we expected.

"We'll have to mitigate the sentence," I whispered to Thomas.

Marianne ran over to Oscar and put her arm around his shoulder. "Don't cry, Oscar," she said warmly. "We will find another punishment for you. Would you rather peel potatoes?"

"Yes, yes!" sobbed Oscar.

"All right, then," said Thomas, and put out his hand to him. "If you promise to behave, Oscar, we might even make you a captain of the Security Guard someday."

"Gee, thanks," said Oscar with an uncertain grin, eagerly grasping Thomas's hand.

"Hurrah!" called the children, happy over the outcome. But suddenly they stopped short. Through the windows came the sound of church bells—the signal that our parents had been sighted. The silence turned into a deafening roar of shouting and laughter. "Our parents are coming! Our parents are coming!" Beside themselves with excitement, they ran pell-mell toward the exits of the Arena.

22

"Oh, Heavenly Day!"

Boy, were we glad to see our parents back again! They had gone straight to Old Square. They had not encountered a single child, but they did hear the bells ring. On the corner of Main Street they stopped short, completely surprised.

We had made some plans for welcoming them when they returned. Our sentries had spied them quite far off, so we had about an hour to prepare for their arrival. Now the smallest children stood in the middle of the square, holding long paper streamers. We had hung flags from the windows of the Town Hall, and above the statue we had strung a banner on which we had scrawled in bold letters, "Welcome home, Dear Parents."

When our parents reached the square, the school band struck up the "March of the Gladiators," and the girls from the church choir sang "Oh, Heavenly Day!" Rita had dressed Lotti and Lisa in their Sun-

day best, and they handed Mayor Lomser two bunches of field daisies, which were the only flowers we could pick in a hurry.

When the hymn had ended, Thomas called out in ringing tones, "Three cheers for our parents!"

"Hip hip *hurrah!* Hip hip *hurrah!* Hip hip *hurrah!*" roared the children in unison.

"Dear children," Mayor Lomser began. He was visibly touched. "Dear children, I thank you on behalf of all the parents. We are very happy to find everything looking so neat and tidy. We expected to find an awful mess—" That was as far as he got. I suspect that he was just warming up for a long speech, but our parents could no longer contain themselves. Paying no further attention to Mr. Lomser, they rushed toward their children to hug and kiss them. There were laughter and tears of joy.

Thomas was beaming all over. His father, not normally demonstrative, had planted a kiss on his cheek. Mark clutched his mother as if he would never let her go. Even Oscar managed a big grin, because his father, the butcher, had affectionately given him a poke in the ribs. Or maybe he was just grinning because he wouldn't have to peel three hundred and forty-seven potatoes.

Marianne and I hurled ourselves at our parents as soon as we discovered them in the mob. They were standing close together near the statue, peering anxiously about. My mother hugged me so hard that my eyeglasses got knocked onto the pavement, where they smashed to smithereens. I didn't care, because I knew that my father would get me new ones.

"There you are at last!" cried Marianne, beside herself with joy, flinging both arms around her father's neck. "Where have you been all this time?"

Mr. Jansen hugged her tight, then planted her in front of him and looked at her tenderly. "Just imagine, Marianne. We were arrested as smugglers!"

"How on earth did that happen?"

"We had gone deep into the forest to give you rascals a good scare. We meant to come back the same night, but we lost our way and crossed the frontier by mistake. All of a sudden we were surrounded by foreign soldiers! They arrested us and locked us up because we had no proper identification papers."

"Why didn't you tell them that you were just trying to scare us?"

"They wouldn't believe us, my dear. It wasn't until today that they finally let us go. You can imagine how fast we came back through the woods after that experience! We were worried to death about you children all the time."

"That serves you right," Marianne said, with a smile. "You must never desert us again."

"I am sure it will never be necessary again," replied Mr. Jansen.

"Darling, we must go home now," said Marianne's mother, taking her hand. "It's late, and tomorrow you must start school again."

"How wonderful!" Marianne sighed happily. "And there will be blueberry muffins for breakfast!"

Henry Winterfeld (1901–1990) was born in Germany. He began writing for children in 1933, when he wrote *Trouble at Timpetill* to entertain his son, who was sick with scarlet fever. He went on to write a number of children's books, which have been published around the world.